REDEMPTION

JOSEPH P. GARLAND

DERMODYHOUSE.COM

DERMODY
HOUSE
PUBLISHING

DERMODYHOUSE.COM

Introduction

THIS STORY IS in two parts.

Part one centers on the relationship between Peter Edgar and Amy Reid, with a few detours along the way.

Part two is about Bridget Casey and Evelyn Manners, and others in Peter and Amy's world. **The story contains a few explicit scenes of both straight and lesbian sex.**

Special thanks to my sister, Liz Sauer, who provided invaluable insights with respect to many aspects of the book.

Part 1

1.

PETER EDGAR WAS RICH. More than comfortably rich. Well more.

He'd grown up as the second son and last child of Michael and Carly Edgar in a wealthy San Francisco suburb. He was two years younger than his brother Ted.

Being second, though, was a safe place to be. His brother had a natural charm and athleticism. By high school, he'd become the handsome one with a good head for figures. For all that, he was never an asshole and when necessary protected his more introverted younger brother. He followed in their father's and his mother's footsteps and went to Stanford.

Although Peter did not appreciate it at the time, when Ted carried the family name to college in Palo Alto, he had the freedom to go elsewhere. Elsewhere turned out to be Morningside Heights in Manhattan. There, Peter settled comfortably at Columbia College, majoring in history.

That was where matters stood with the Edgar clan until Peter was a sophomore. That's when things changed wildly. Years earlier, his father had been recruited by some Stanford classmates to leave his cushy job at the venture capital firm Andreessen Horowitz and throw his lot in with a start-up. They were engineers and he was a finance geek and they built that new company, Palix Corp., into a unicorn, that is, a company with a billion-dollar valuation.

When it went public, Michael Edgar suddenly was beyond rich. Peter had by then gotten his BA at Columbia and his brother Ted was doing very well with his own Stanford MBA at a San Francisco hedge fund.

Peter's parents were indulgent enough to have paid his tuition and expenses at Columbia and to have bought him a two-bedroom condo apartment in a high rise at the corner of East 70th and First Avenue. On his own merits, he got an analyst's job at XTach, yet another start-up, this one with its headquarters in Manhattan's Meatpacking District downtown.

And there matters stood for Peter Edgar as he grew into his position at the company. He soon joined XTach's tradition of four or five officemates heading out after work to a tavern on 13th Street for burgers and fries and Brooklyn-brewed beers. In early March 2019 when Peter had been at the company for almost a year, four of them were at a round table with their IPAs waiting for their burgers when a breaking news story appeared on those of the muted TV monitors spread about the restaurant and bar that were not showing ESPN.

It was a video of a fire truck, one of those yellow airport ones, spraying foam on the wreckage of a jet. The chryon read that it was an accident in Aspen. *No survivors. Cause unknown* ended the message which appeared again and again beneath the wreckage footage and talking heads on CNBC.

Peter and the others stared at it and were chilled by the hope no one had suffered too much before they died. That's when their food arrived, and they turned their now more sober attention to that and to the second round of the Brooklyn Brews they'd ordered.

About ten minutes later, Peter felt a hand on his shoulder. He looked up and saw their boss.

"Peter," he said, "can I have a word?" His voice was missing the natural confidence it normally had. A very discombobulated Peter followed him, each of his colleagues glad it wasn't them, to a small alcove near the front door where a stranger in a suit and tie stood stiffly watching the two men approach.

"Are you Peter Edgar?" he asked. Peter said he was.

The stranger discreetly displayed an NYPD Detective shield and said point blank, "there's no easy way to say this, sir, but your parents and your brother were killed in that plane crash in Aspen." He nodded toward the scene of the Colorado runway playing on CNBC with cuts to talking heads in a studio.

2.

IT HAD BEEN THE family's leased Gulfstream G650. The NTSB concluded that the jet had caught a sudden windshear on its final approach to the Aspen Airport. Peter's parents and his brother as well as his brother's partner (who Peter was looking forward to meeting when the family came to New York in early June) were among the seven who died on impact. *God, those final moments* haunted Peter, especially in the silence before he finally fell asleep each night.

But needs must. Peter took two weeks' bereavement leave to bury his family excepting his father's mother, who lived in a Marin County nursing home. Grandma Edgar walked through the horrible funeral service with its three coffins in the church in Palo Alto. She gripped Peter's arm and the two of them walked slowly to the gravesite following the train of hearses. The cemetery was outside San Francisco.

The next day, Peter met with the family's lawyers in the city itself.

He was informed that he was suddenly very wealthy. It'd be a while before the formalities were completed but when they were, in addition to the generous trust fund established for Grandma Edgar, Peter would have hundreds of millions in liquid assets and own a house in Palo Alto, a Georgian townhouse in London's Belgravia, and two additional properties in New York.

The first New York place was a five-bedroom condo on the ninth floor of a pre-war building on the east side of Park Avenue in the seventies. The other was the modern mansion in East Hampton on New York's Long Island that a Madoff victim had put up. It had a view over the beach and to the Atlantic and even a thirty-step staircase that went from its deck to the beach itself. After Peter's parents had bought it, the family regularly held get togethers there and it was where Peter took some of his vacation time.

Once he got titles, Peter sold the California place but kept the others. He moved the few blocks to the big place on Park. He upgraded his wardrobe and found a bespoke tailor on the second floor of a French boutique on Madison Avenue and a custom shoemaker a few blocks south of that. And he flew Grandma Edgar to an exclusive care facility in Bridgehampton, only a few miles from the house.

He made a point of visiting her every few weeks. It was a fine, private facility, and his grandmother had what amounted to her own little hotel suite. She made an effort to waddle out with her walker as much as she could, including for daily meals and evening entertainments. Often, she went alone with her podcasts and audiobooks to one of the chairs that were sprinkled about the enclosed courtyard where visitors would sit with residents, as Peter often did with her.

She was happy there, or at least as happy as someone in her limited physical condition could be even though her old friends, those who were still alive, were all out in northern California where she and her husband had raised Michael, their only son, who was such a point of pride when he'd gotten into Stanford. And that pride extended to both of her grandsons and their academic and other achievements. Her great regret was that she was running out of friends to show pictures to.

As for the family's Columbia grad, he still worked at XTach after he became wealthy. While a few of his professional colleagues suddenly discovered that they had a great friendship with the analyst, most of his true

5

friends had the *that's-cool* attitude about Peter so things with them changed remarkably little, although those closest to him did not object when Peter insisted on picking up the check when they all went out.

Peter had been keeping a utilitarian dark gray Audi Q5 in a garage near his building for ease of heading east, but with some measure of guilt he decided to splurge. The result was a dark blue Aston Martin DB11 convertible with a deep cream interior and a special-order mustard yellow Porsche Cayenne with a black interior. Suddenly, most weekends found him driving one or the other the hundred miles or so to the Hamptons house. The poor Audi became the house car.

The sizes of the house and the apartment were sometimes disconcerting to Peter. They heightened the loneliness he sometimes felt, especially when he sat on the Hamptons deck overlooking the Atlantic and lost himself in the roar of the waves hitting the sand in thoughts of what was to come.

He missed his family. He'd reminisce out loud about the times he sat on this deck with his parents and Ted in these same comfortable chairs under the same shielding umbrella and the expensive vintage reds being swirled in a glass. It was then, more than at any other times, that he struggled, never not noticing the irony of it all, of him owning all of this because they were gone.

He began ferrying friends he had picked up at work in the Porsche for week-ends in his little slice of Paradise. And they were good friends who teased him about continuing to work when he could spend his time at the beach or in the elite neighborhoods and restaurants of London or pretty much anywhere else he wanted to go with pretty much any gorgeous woman he wanted to go—or *come*, one friend said naughtily—with.

Peter laughed it off but in the end it highlighted how uncertain he was about what he wanted to do with his life.

Back in Manhattan, he had easily slipped into the life of a rich New Yorker existing on family wealth. He, or more precisely his money and passably good looks, attracted the attention of tall, beautiful single women who, as Austen would have put it, were themselves in want of a wealthy husband. As a rule, one such lady accompanied him on the charity fund raisers at the museums and ballrooms that littered Manhattan and were sprinkled about Brooklyn and the in-season ones in the mansions in the ~~more~~ most exclusive communities in the Hamptons to which he was suddenly invited. It wasn't long before his presence on the A-list circuit received attention in *The Times* and *The Post* and in innumerable gossip blogs and Instagram posts. Even *The Wall Street Journal* wanted to do a piece on New York's *sudden socialite*, but he declined the interview request.

He might not be particularly happy but he was never alone.

Then in August about a year-and-a-half after the Gulfstream crash, an awful weather forecast deterred his usual trip to East Hampton. He substituted a rain-soaked Saturday six-mile run on the Central Park Drive and spent the afternoon doing some reading in his apartment before buying an overpriced ticket for an off-Broadway show he'd wanted to see. He enjoyed it.

He got home early and, alone, microwaved something Mexican from the freezer to keep body and soul together. With that done, he poured himself a couple of fingers of Johnnie Walker Black over ice in an etched Waterford crystal tumbler and settled into the library.

The old room had become his refuge. His father had never gotten around to upgrading it, though he had for most of the apartment's other rooms, the library and, strangely, master bedroom being the exceptions. Those other rooms would make a fine house porn spread in *Architectural Digest*, the library would fit perfectly into *American Heritage*. The Gilded Age issue.

It retained the *faux* charm of a Belgravian gentleman's sanctuary. Shelf after shelf of unopened leather-bound books, the walls painted a hunter's green. The antique sense of most of the shelves was broken only by several filled with modern and recent editions that he actually read.

The most attractive spot in the room was a window that looked out over 75th Street with a cushioned windowseat and a pair of wingback chairs on either side and a small, mahogany scalloped table between them.

Peter, that night, put his Scotch-filled Waterford on a coaster on the table before taking a turn around the room in the slight illumination of wall sconces. Here and there he slid a volume out. There was no dust; the cleaning crew that came in every Tuesday and Friday made sure to dust in the unlikely event that someone would actually remove a book.

He carried one of those recent novels, one he'd ordered after a fawning review on the front page of *The Times Book Review*, to the wing chair to the left of the window but when he'd settled into the too comfortable chair, he put the volume on his lap and let his mind wander outside. The storm had passed. The Manhattan sky never truly turns black, and that night it had an inky darkness with threads of magically illuminated clouds racing west-to-east.

In the morning, the sky was clear and very blue. The temperature was already in the low 80s, but the dank humidity of Saturday was gone. Clarity and clearness remained in its wake. After another six-mile loop of the

Park and a shower, Peter headed out for a lone brunch at a small place on the south side of 79th. It was all part of his normal routine when he was alone in the city for the weekend.

3.

AMY ELIZABETH REID HAD absentmindedly stopped in the middle of the Park Avenue sidewalk about a block north of Peter's condo to adjust the grip on her bag when he plowed right into her.

She turned to glare at the asshole who'd nearly knocked her to the ground even as he reached to stabilize her. They faced each other.

She did not recognize him, notwithstanding his notoriety in the society pages of the high-brow and low-brow publications and websites that were the lifeblood of curious New York.

What she saw instead was a more than marginally handsome man, five-ten and well-built in tailored khaki pants with a well-defined crease and a blue Brooks Brothers polo. Brown Italian loafers without socks and a worn blue Columbia cap. She liked what she could see of his hair. It was a dark brown with a bit of curl and long enough to feel playful in one's fingers but not *too* reckless. He quickly removed his Wayfarers.

What *he* saw was a more than marginally pretty twenty-something in a yellow sundress with flickers of red and blue flowers on green stems. Her light brown hair was in a ponytail corralled by a red hair band.

When they had both regained their bearings and stood facing each other, they exchanged simultaneous apologies.

"Don't be daft," she said. "I was the idiot who just stopped."

"No, no. I was scrolling and not paying attention. It was my bad." Peter continued. "Look. Can we settle this at brunch?"

"That's your pick-up line?" she asked with a grin. "How's that running into women on the sidewalk thing working for you?"

Seeing his reaction to this tease, she quickly added, "Just kidding. I'd love to but I don't have time."

"Some other time, maybe," he said, but she quickly said she'd be happy to share a quick coffee. After he took a look at the empty ring finger on her left hand, a peek that she noticed, they agreed to something at the Starbucks a block east on Lexington.

The walk itself proved a delight. They went side-by-side, a close but appropriate distance between them. She found out how long he'd lived in Manhattan and he found out the same about her. He found out that she worked in a PR firm in midtown and she learned that he worked at a tech start-up in the Meatpacking District though, he hastened to add, he was not himself a tech guy. "Just a BA in history," he admitted.

The Starbucks itself was typically crowded for a Sunday morning, and after she'd gotten her latte and he'd picked up a straight coffee, they had to wait a few minutes, nervously rocking slightly as they did, until a table by the window overlooking 77th Street opened up.

The store was its standard-issue dark with the smell—or *aroma*?—of bitter caffeine and the constant din of patrons and baristas wafting around and people waiting to use the bathroom. As for Amy and Peter, they remained at their table long after their coffees were gone.

They had fallen into a relaxed conversation, one that almost seemed like a catching up between long-lost friends. She told of her local background. Brought up and going to college less than twenty-five miles to the north. Enjoying her work in PR. Her folks still living in Westchester County and her only brother Brian with a Congressional staff position in DC.

11

He was trying not to boast about his Columbia degree and offered only vague stories of his California background and having lost his parents and only sibling in a plane crash. That last hit her, and she said how sorry she was and they left it at that.

He kept the details of who they were and how they'd died and especially what he'd inherited from the conversation. She plainly had no idea who he was, he realized, and he had no intention of educating her.

Amy didn't notice that her companion had been noticed and that others were taking what they thought were discreet pictures of the person they sort of recognized as being famous for something but not knowing what that might be. Peter was used to the attention. He ignored it. He and Amy, though, could not long ignore the glares directed their way from other customers. Not caring a whit for who they were. Caring about getting their table.

When Amy realized it, she mentioned it to Peter and the pair sheepishly collected their empty cups, used a napkin to tidy up the table, and were soon on the street.

Time had flowed quickly. Too quickly. Amy was shocked that she was already late for the meeting she'd dressed up for. She told Peter she had to be off and after sending an apologetic text to her friend, she stepped onto Lexington Avenue to hail a cab south. One pulled up almost immediately and as he held the door open for her, Peter asked if they might meet for coffee again. To the annoyed impatience of the cabbie, she put her number in his phone and he put his in hers.

"I'd like that," she said as he closed the door.

"I'd like that," he called softly to the taxi as it merged into southbound traffic. And sitting in the back of the cab with her phone cradled in her palm and his number staring back at her, Amy's first thought was that she hoped he'd call. There was something about him. A sweetness. A kindness. Sure, he was decked out in high-end clothes on a Sunday morning with a hint of the Eastern establishment with a northern California vibe but he was without pretense.

Yes. She would like to see him again. It wasn't because of his trappings of wealth. She had no idea who he was. She didn't read *The Post* and skipped *The Times*'s society page She was very familiar with social media as part of her job in PR, but the intricacies that seemed to absorb a disproportionate share of the internet world's bandwidth were beyond her. She could literally run into Kim Kardasian's butt on a Park Avenue sidewalk and not have a clue as to who, or what, it was attached to.

4.

WHILE AMY WAS GETTING ready to go to work on Monday, rain started pelting against the window of her one-bedroom midblock walkup on 80th between Second and Third. She generally enjoyed the two mile or so walk south to her office on East 40th, but not in this monsoon. Before leaving, she took a final look at the sky. It was gray on gray and the water was unrelenting as it battered her windows. It was not letting up any time soon.

She threw a rain slicker over her dress and grabbed a too-small retractable umbrella from a hook in the closet by the door and ventured out, leaning forward into the rain as she slogged with a parade of others doing precisely the same along the drenched and puddled sidewalk to the steps that took her to the subway at Lex and 77th Street, right at the corner where the Starbucks stood. The umbrella had done little to protect her so she was left dripping in a dress that was wet below the slicker's protection and drenched sneakers—she'd change at the office—on the platform for the southbound Number 6 train towards Grand Central.

As Peter Edgar had observed in his study of her at Starbucks the day before, Amy was shorter than average and lighter than average. Her face was round and her hazel eyes set a hair closer to one another than average. Her lips were slightly large yet had something that made them inviting. Her hair was light brown and long. On the whole, it was an above-average face. She had a row of three piercings on her left ear and two on her right.

She was an example of the whole being greater than the sum of her parts.

As Peter Edgar had *not* yet had a full opportunity to observe, Amy Reid was also very smart. She had worked at her public relations firm since she'd graduated a few years earlier from a small liberal arts college in Purchase, New York in Westchester. It was not far from the suburb just north of the city where she grew up as the only daughter and where she still spent Christmas and Thanksgivings and birthdays, with her parents and usually with her brother Brian, who'd Amtrak up from Washington.

And as Peter Edgar had had the opportunity to observe, she was neither married nor engaged.

But all of that hardly mattered in this Monday's shitty weather. She wasn't a big fan of Mondays as a general rule but even less so in weather like that morning's. She stood in the middle of the southbound subway platform with bits of rain dripping down through the grates along the sidewalk above. It was as close to the tracks as she could get, and there was barely room to breathe as those in the crowd crushed themselves together. Politely.

The first train pulled in. It was far too crowded, though, for any more than twenty or so of those waiting to themselves squeeze on board. As that train pulled away, Amy and the others who'd been left behind filled the space those fortunate ones had vacated. She hoped that the second train would be the charm.

And it was. She was near the car's door when it opened and pushed her way in after those getting out had done so. She turned to get somewhat down the center aisle and with one hand clutched the metal floor-to-ceiling pole. Her hand was joined by several others on the pole, each diplomatically the slightest distance away from the others.

After the familiar *stand clear of the closing doors, please* announcement, the doors did close and the train began to move with a jolt that shook everyone. They were all well accustomed to the train's launch and they responded like a choreographed flashmob.

Her car fell into its rhythm but only briefly. It had barely gotten up to speed when it began to slow as it entered the 68th Street station, where the same ritual and the same *stand clear of the closing doors, please* announcement that had taken place less than half-a-mile earlier at 77th was repeated. Amy held her position at her pole, doing the subway rider's gyrations to allow people getting off to maneuver around her.

When the trip resumed, she let her mind wander in time with the car's hypnotic movement. It was a quiet, communal car. Almost all of the other riders were doing what she was doing or staring at their tablets or phones except for three girls in Catholic school uniforms who were gabbing at the other end of the car.

After this stop-and-go ritual was repeated at several stations, the train pulled into Grand Central. Amid several shouts of *coming through*, Amy joined the line that left the car and across the damp platform to one of the many staircases that rose up. She climbed the first flight like one of a pack of horny salmon heading upstream. At its top, she joined the mayhem of commuters and students racing in all directions, zigging and zagging around awed tourists to get to the 4, 5, 6, or 7 trains or to rush down a tiled hallway that would bring them to the Shuttle, a train that went back and forth between Grand Central and Times Square, back-and-forth, back-and-forth, all day and all night long.

Through the turnstile using only her hip to push it out of the way, Amy walked up a final flight of steps, dry until nearly the top one, patiently waiting for the three or four ahead of her to get their umbrellas open, as she was to do when her turn came.

The rain was now hard but not as brutal as it had been when she'd hurried from her apartment to the subway and she joined the flow south to 40th and after the light on Park changed she walked the block-and-a-half to her building on Madison.

She closed and shook her dripping umbrella. The lobby floor was damp from those who had preceded her. She fished her ID card from her shoulder bag and pushed through a turnstile and onto a thankfully empty elevator that would zip her up to her office on the 23rd floor, to Enswich & Taylor, her PR firm.

This is how work began, though not always in a physical atmosphere as dank and damp as it was that day. Before getting her coffee from the kitchen and bringing it to her cubicle, she went to the ladies' and did what she could with paper towels to rid herself of the rain and sweat that had encased her from the trip.

Not so bad, considering, she told herself when she looked in the mirror, but she'd have to brush out her hair as soon as she could. She settled into her little black chair with a sigh and took her pair of dry work pumps from her drawer and put them on before booting her computer and letting the angst of her short commute dissipate.

Amy loved her job. She liked the people with whom she worked. They were smart and pleasant people from New York and pretty much everywhere else. She liked the work itself.

As she got herself settled in at her desk that Monday, she lost herself in that work and when she looked up from her computer it was already eleven. On the way to getting a coffee refill, she glanced through a conference room window. The rain had stopped. By lunchtime, it'd be dry enough, if muggy, for lunch in Bryant Park.

Bryant Park is the great oasis in midtown Manhattan. Its central lawn spreads out to the west of the library, the

17

one with Patience and Fortitude, its famous lions. That greenery is surrounded by walkways lined with small green round tables and chairs and, best of all, a potpourri of Manhattan workers who fill them.

With all that rain, it wasn't as crowded as it would normally be on an August Monday at noontime, and the lawn itself was cordoned off because of the wetness. With a salad and the iced tea she'd picked up in a fancy place on Fifth, she wandered in and quickly found a table and dry chair that overlooked the lawn.

Amy allowed her thoughts to wander as she chomped on the greens and beans and other things tossed in her salad, alternating with sips of her iced tea. With the sounds from the other visitors and from traffic passing along 42nd Street muffled in the humid air, she sat in her solitude and her thoughts perhaps inevitably drifted to the stranger she'd met only the afternoon before. To Peter Edgar.

There was something vaguely familiar about him but she couldn't put her finger on it. He was handsome in a spoiled rich kid sort of way yet there was nothing dickish or off-putting about him. To the contrary.

To be sure, Amy didn't have a lot of experience with men, handsome or otherwise. Mark Astor had extended from her final semester at Manhattanville to her early months in the city but his attentions turned to someone he met during orientation for his job at Chase. After him, she'd hooked up now and then with guys she'd met as part of a Thursday night pub crawl she got dragged on with Sarah, a friend from work, and one and sometimes two of Sarah's Sarah Lawrence buddies.

Ray Connors was a little on the short side and had a great sense of humor but he only made it to two months before they began losing interest in one another.

Gerry Phillips was her last relationship that was in any way *serious* but he started emitting bad, controlling vibes after they'd slept together a few times. She started ignoring his calls and texts until she got the courage, or at least a piece of courage, to call him and say they should start seeing other people.

Amy was depressed about her prospects. But not so depressed that she didn't enjoy exchanging touches with a sweet young lawyer named Dan three weeks later after they met on one of the Sarah-led crawls she'd skipped when she was exclusive with Gerry. She hadn't yet recovered her confidence in the complicated world of twenty-something singledom in Manhattan and while she was telling herself that she was content to just ride it out and rely on chance, having become fully capable of taking care of certain needs without the necessity of a man's involvement, she could not escape a certain internal gnawing.

This was in the recesses of her mind when Peter Edgar had leapt to its forefront. Something about him ignited something she'd place aside after Gerry. He was self-effacing yet confident. More than average looking, yes, but his pieces fit very well together.

As her thoughts progressed, she found herself imagining how they—she and he—would literally fit well together.

As had happened at the Starbucks on Lex, time had slipped away and she was hit by the reality of having to get back to her office. She took the last of her salad and had a final sip of her iced tea and headed from the park.

5.

PETER SLEPT POORLY THAT Sunday night. It wasn't just the rain that moved in overnight and was splattering against his bedroom windows much as it was doing not so far away at Amy's. No. It *was* Amy.

As soon as he was home on Sunday afternoon, never having actually gotten brunch, he'd booted up his laptop and did some sleuthing. His subject: Amy Reid. And he found...virtually nothing. As far as he could tell, zero Facebook or Twitter or Instagram presence. He got some basics via LinkedIn: Graduate of Manhattanville College, 2020, BFA, The first Covid year. Art History. That made her two years younger than him. Worked at Enswich & Taylor. He'd never heard of it but got the basics from its website. Small public relations firm that specialized in crisis management. Which he assumed meant fixing inappropriate social media posts or late-night rendezvouses caught in a paparazzo's lens.

Still. That was neither here nor there. That morning, facing the same rain that Amy Reid was dealing with on her hurried walk to the 6 Train, a doorman held a large black umbrella over him and then held open the door of the cab that would take Peter through the chaos of a wet Manhattan rush hour south to XTach's headquarters. Once there, he raced through the rain and was quickly inside. This was hardly the midtown office building with all its security protocols of the sort Amy had to deal with. It was open and industrial in an almost throwback way. Peter took the wide staircase from the lobby two steps at a time to the third floor and the firm's main office.

Once he was settled at his cubicle with a coffee and bagel with cream cheese he got from XTach's small kitchen, he chastised himself for having perhaps spent too much time thinking of Amy Reid since he very much doubted that she had given a moment's thought to him. He didn't know her type but was pretty sure he was not hers since he was, more than anything, the asshole who'd bashed into her on the sidewalk. She'd given him her number, but he knew that it was best to wait, if he was going to call her at all. She had *his* number so maybe the better move would be to wait until she called him. He didn't know.

He told himself that he should focus on Thursday's Whitney Museum fund raiser and particularly Cheryl Evans, who a friend had arranged to accompany him to the gala and perhaps for a post-event dinner at his place. The friend had texted Cheryl's photo, and he expected he'd be quite up for a post-gala meal with her.

With that mental clarification and the storm harmlessly in its final throes outside, he was able to enjoy what was another of XTach's traditions. A bunch of pies with a variety of toppings were ordered from a pizzeria on Hudson Street and by noon their boxes were spread next to one another on the large conference room's long credenza that usually witnessed less *fun* lunches. Off to one side was a stack of paper plates and napkins and on the other a collection of sodas and other (non-alcoholic) drinks. Peter loved how the communal meal brought together the disparate parts of the company, even if only for an hour or so.

No one knew that he was funding it all.

6.

NEW YORK'S WEATHER MAY not be as changeable as Dublin's, but it can sometimes give the Irish capital a run for its money. So it was that Tuesday, the sky a brilliant blue and all signs indicating that it would grow into a beautiful not-too-hot, not-too-humid day.

It was quite natural, then, that Amy and Sarah from work would buy their salads at the place on Fifth across from the library and eat in Bryant Park.

After they'd collected their mixed salads and drinks, they followed scores of similar midtowners into the park and were lucky enough to catch a couple leaving a table and chairs in the shade of one of the trees that lined the southern border, within earshot of the melody that played on the nearby carousel. They grabbed it to the consternation of another couple approaching from the west, but a wee bit too far away. Like parking on the street in New York, being close is not good enough.

As Amy and Sarah were sitting down, Amy mentioned with a hint of enthusiasm that she'd met *someone*. It had been a while since she'd said that to anyone, including herself.

"What do you mean *met someone*?" Sarah asked as she arranged her lunch on her side of the green mesh table.

Once Amy had her own salad and iced tea set on the table, she told Sarah about being bumped into by a nice-looking guy on Sunday and enjoying sitting with him at Starbucks for coffees and apologies.

"Holy meet-cute," Sarah said with a laugh. "Tell me about him."

Amy realized bringing it up was not the smartest thing since nothing was, she knew, going to come of it, but she'd started and was bound to answer Sarah's question.

"He just seems like a really nice guy. Smart. Well dressed. I think he actually listened to what I had to say. Stuff like that."

"The type you'd bring home to your parents?"

"I met him , Sarah," Amy laughed. "Don't start shopping for you maid-of-honor dress just yet."

"Can I at least Google it?"

"Jesus, Sarah," Amy was able to say to her friend.

"Okay, okay." She paused. "Looks?"

"You know I'm not so superficial," Amy said with a sweet laugh. "Seriously, he's a fine specimen of a man."

Now they both laughed.

"He really is." Amy used the plastic fork to take a bite of her salad.

"Honey," Sarah said, her own fork midway between the clear plastic container and her mouth and turning more serious, "you deserve one of the good ones."

Which was true after the stories she'd heard from Amy of some of her prior liaisons, even the longer (in time if not necessarily otherwise) ones, like Gerry. The last weeks with him had been...difficult and the two women often spoke about it and in time were both glad she'd parted ways with him and over more time they reached a consensus that Amy had *dodged a bullet*.

But Gerry was well and forever in her past and, Amy was led to believe, in some other east sider's present. She was strangely excited about talking instead about this stranger who she had passed like he was just another ship in the night.

"You exchanged numbers?" The question brought Amy back to Planet Earth.

Amy admitted that they had.

"Good. So, what's his name and how cute is he?" Sarah asked. She took another bite of her Romaine.

Amy said he was called Peter Edgar and before she could continue, Sarah's fork had dropped into her salad.

"*The* Peter Edgar?" she asked, looking hard at her friend.

"Just Peter Edgar as far as I know. He's a couple of years older, according to what he told me. Works at some tech company in the West Village. Why?"

Sarah pulled her phone from her bag and her index finger started racing over the screen, her salad ignored. Amy stared at her in confusion. After about thirty seconds, her friend held her phone up, its screen facing Amy, and said, "This him?"

Amy was surprised. "Yeah, that's him. Why?"

"Amy, I love you but you really need to get out more." She pulled her phone back and her fingers were rocketing across the screen. "Read this."

Taking the phone, Amy saw a Wikipedia entry. For *the* Peter Edgar. Scooting to Personal Information, she read,

> *A real catch, he is known for being a ladies' man although learning who his particular femme de jour is has long proved difficult. He's never been connected to any one woman in particular. He is seen regularly being adorned with a celebrity or model at one of Manhattan's or the Hamptons' charity fêtes.*

Sarah turned her phone back to herself. More scrolling. After several moments, she said, "Oh, shit" and again handed the phone to Amy. Who saw a photo of herself sitting with the Peter Edgar at Starbucks on Sunday. It linked to a Page Six story on *The Post*'s website:

The One? Peter Edgar gazing longingly into the eyes of an unknown "companion" at a Starbucks on Lex this past Sunday. Is it finally "her"?

With a quiet *fuck,* Amy practically threw the phone back at Sarah and looked around the park.

"No. No. No," she repeated when her eyes returned to her slightly eaten lunch. "I don't understand." She looked right at Sarah. "I do not want to be in *The Post*. Ever."

She paused.

"Is there anything I can do? I don't want paparazzi following me around." She scanned all the faces nearby of strangers sitting at tables or walking past oblivious to the little drama being played out at Amy's table. "I don't want strangers to stare at me, pointing to me, hitting me up for money they think I have."

She grabbed her salad and snapped the top on and put the cap on the iced tea and shoved them into the paper bag from the eatery. Before Sarah could react and recover from being stunned by the Page Six photo still on her phone, Amy was up and gone, dropping the lunch bag into a bin by the park's entrance. Her friend caught her just as she'd reached Fifth Avenue. Sarah ran her arm through Amy's and they returned to the office without saying anything to one another.

Meanwhile, a few miles to the south, Peter Edgar himself was having difficulty concentrating. Which was strange. He had long been able to compartmentalize, to perform the task-at-hand without regard for interruptions. It was a useful skill, particularly when one's office is a cubicle among a swarm of coding bees. But he couldn't get that girl out of his head.

He pulled his phone out for the umpteenth time with thoughts of calling her, but he resisted the temptation. In a strange way, he felt that she was out of his league. She was completely different and by any objective if superficial physical standard was lightyears from the women he'd appeared with at events and often hooked up with.

She was completely different from anyone he'd met since becoming rich.

"Yo, Peter," Chris, another analyst called to him. "Check out *The Post*. Page Six."

By the time he had, the other was at his cubicle.

"She's kind of cute, mate," he said. "Anything happening there?"

Peter looked up. "I don't really know her. I ran into her near my apartment, literally, and we just had coffee so we could apologize to each other and then she was gone."

"Tell me you at least got her number."

Peter thought of the entry on his phone. "Yeah, but I probably won't call her. I kind of lied when I didn't tell her how...well off I am."

"I don't know, man. If I had your bank account I'd fucking tattoo it on my forehead." Peter ignored this.

Chris took another look at the photo on his own phone.

"Seriously. I don't know. You both look really relaxed here, like I don't know if I've ever seen you like before. Like old friends. You know?"

"Maybe."

"No *maybe*. Just do it. You can afford to pay for the call." He laughed as he turned to get back to his own desk and Peter wondered if he was right. *What do I have to lose?*

Fuck he thought. He'd made a concerted effort to keep his true identity from her. *Would she think he lied and end it before it got started?*

He went to the conference room where they'd all had that pizza the day before. He closed the door and dialed her number.

"Hi," she said, her voice flat.

"This is Peter, Peter Edgar, from Sunday," he said.

"I know. I recognized the number."

There was a pause. A brief one while he mustered his courage, nervous about where this conversation would be going.

She jumped in. "I, you know, I found out about you."

"From *The Post*?"

"Yeah. And then Wikipedia. It was quite revealing."

"I guess I should have told you. I'm sorry that I didn't. And that you got your photo everywhere."

"Look. You couldn't know that someone took that picture or that *The Post* would be interested in it."

"It's now all over the internet," he regretted to say.

"Great. I'm going to be a meme."

She was not happy and it was his fault. She kind of understood but, still, it was all a bit much. Now from what she'd read, he really wasn't much of a celebrity. He'd not done anything to make anyone care the least bit about him except for the accident of being the only surviving child of a wildly rich man who died in a Gulfstream crash on approach to the Aspen Airport.

But he was young enough and handsome enough and available enough to create a swell of envy in man and woman alike so he was going to be a target at least for a while. As he was speaking to Amy, he understood that he had developed a thick skin about it but she'd been thrown straight to the lions and she didn't deserve that.

He ended the call to say he'd try to figure out what to do to protect her.

Amy wasn't waiting. Crisis management, after all, was her job, even a crisis that barely spread beyond one degree of recognition.

Sarah wasn't surprised when Amy looked at her over the cubicle's four-foot wall and said they needed to talk in the privacy of the conference room. Once there, Sarah closed the door.

"It's not good," Sarah said. "The good-old Reddit sleuths have outed you." She turned her tablet so Amy could see. There it was, not only the Starbucks picture but something someone scraped from her Manhattanville yearbook and the stiff one she'd posted on LinkedIn.

"Not your best pictures," Sarah said, attempting without success to lighten the matter.

Amy dropped into one of the conference room's chairs. "I need to speak with Evan," she said. Evan Taylor was their boss.

"*We* need to," Sarah corrected and within a minute they were both in comfortable chairs in their boss's corner office and Sarah was showing him the details on her tablet.

"Amy," he said when he'd digested what he'd seen. "The most important question is whether you want to try for some sort of relationship with this"—he looked at the article—"Peter Edgar guy. If not, it'll blow over when people realize you are not—what did *The Post* say?"

"The one," Sarah answered.

"Yes. *The one.* A gala with his typical blonde with legs that are forever long and...boobs trying to escape from her cleavage will take care of it. So?"

Amy thought for a moment. She'd not invested anything in him. While it wasn't like she had any other promising alternatives on the horizon, she'd made it this far in her life without him and could put that however enjoyable hour at Starbucks behind her.

"I barely know the guy," she told the others. "All this is too much. No, it's not worth it," she said with finality.

"So that's it, then," Evan said. "You want me to call him?"

Amy breathed a sigh of relief. That was easy, a crisis safely and permanently nipped in the bud. "No," she said to Evan. "I'll do it."

She caucused herself in the conference room, staring out the large window across 40th Street. She made the return call and after a bit of back-and-forth that ended with them agreeing it was for the best and *good lucking* each other about their respective futures, that enjoyable hour at Starbucks was placed somewhere in recesses of each of their memories.

And at the Thursday gala for the Whitney, Peter Edgar appeared with Carolyn Evans, an enhanced blonde who in heels was just his height and after the requisite photos were taken and they sat through the speeches and the chicken dinners, they rode in a car to his place. He hooked up with her primarily if not exclusively to try to flush Amy out of his system and then accompanied her through his building's lobby and to the sidewalk. An Uber was waiting for her there, its back door being held open by Terry, one of the doormen. Peter gave her a slight kiss on the lips before helping her into the Escalade under Terry's watchful and discreet eye.

It was a little past midnight, and Peter watched the SUV head north through the very light traffic to wherever it was that she wished to go.

He was back in his apartment within five minutes and after congratulating himself about how well he'd handled the misdirection from the *Amy Reid situation*, he made himself comfortable in one of the guest rooms, leaving it to the next day's cleaning crew to take care of the disarray in his room and on his bed. They were used to the task, especially on Friday mornings.

In Friday's Page Six, there was a short item in the right-hand column. It had a small photo. The photo was a clear shot of Peter Edgar waving from a red carpet with a tall, elegant blonde on his arm. They were both smiling as they walked through the gaggle of paparazzi. The comments flooded in and virtually all of them agreed that this woman was far more appropriate for the Peter Edgar than Amy Reid could possibly have been.

No, the jury concluded, Amy Reid was not destined to be *the one*.

7

IN THE DAYS AND WEEKS that followed, the glancing connection between Amy Reid and Peter Edgar faded drip-by-drip to become nothing but a pair of fond memories and a cautionary tale. Their lives returned to their normalcy. Amy walked to and from her office when the weather was good. She ate her salad and drank her iced tea at Bryant Park, with Sarah and one or two other workmates as often as not.

She went out on Thursday nights with friends and sometimes brought someone home with her and after a month or so she stopped imagining that it was Peter sharing her bed.

As for him, his image was again being splashed across the usual suspects from events in Manhattan or in the Hamptons. And for him, too, after a month or so he stopped imagining that the woman in his bed was Amy.

On a Thursday in mid-October, while Amy was bar hopping with Sarah, Peter was in a hotel ballroom on East 57th Street. Lenox Hill Hospital was having its annual gala. It was a formal event meant to raise some money and show appreciation for those who'd made substantial gifts to the hospital over the prior twelve months. And Peter was among them, having donated enough to the pediatric cancer wing to have his name placed on a donor-appreciation plaque that visitors saw when they stepped out of the elevator on the fifth floor of Lenox Hill's east wing.

As was usual for such high-end events, lesser doctors and nurses were invited on something of a rotating basis. This time, one of those nurses was Bridget Casey.

As the name suggests, she was half of Irish extraction and, not surprisingly for New York, her father was an NYPD detective and her mother an ER nurse in northern Manhattan.

Bridget had followed in her mother's footsteps. She was an RN at Lenox Hill Hospital on Manhattan's Upper East Side. She was 5' 5" and had a round face and blonde hair kept shoulder length—it reflected her mother's Swedish genes—and round, blue eyes. She lived in the Woodlawn section of the Bronx. It's at the northernmost part of the borough and has long been an Irish-American enclave that extends to bordering Yonkers.

She usually took the Number 4 subway to and from work in the same pediatric cancer department that coincidentally bore the plaque with Peter's name on it. She alternatively loved and hated her job, the hate being from the suffering she witnessed and her inability to do much about it.

Bridget was drafted into going to this Lenox Hill fund-raiser to help put a face on the department's nurses. It had been a long day and she had wanted to get home but she had committed and she'd at least get a good meal and some very good wine for her efforts.

She wore one of the gowns that were shared by the similarly-sized nurses. It was a shimmering blue that didn't quite fit Bridget's curves, but it was close enough to make it acceptable even in the elite couture company in which she'd be mingling and it matched wonderfully with her eyes and the chignon into which a fellow nurse had put her hair during a meal break. She wore her own pair of two-inch heels that she pulled out whenever she had to go to one of these things or a wedding and carried a clutch she'd borrowed from her mother for the occasion.

She took the 103 bus down Lexington, her classy outfit generating her share of notice from the other passengers, and walked the block and a half to the hotel.

The cavernous ballroom on the second floor was beyond tasteful in its decorations. A steady stream of servers in black trousers and white shirts carrying trays with drinks or *hors d'oeuvres* navigated through the gaps between clusters of guests in formal attire and, on the women at least, sparkling jewels. It all reflected the subtle wealth and accomplishment that was and had always been a hallmark of high society in New York.

It was plain that Bridget was not of that society in her ill-fitted gown and lack of diamonds except for the pair of studs in her ears, also borrowed from her mom. Still, at this event she did belong even if she did not fit in. As she stood off the periphery more than a few guests who saw the *RN* on her badge smiled and nodded at her as they passed, some even stopping to express their appreciation for her work.

One who noticed the department in which she worked stepped close to her and reached for her hand. She was a pretty woman in her late 40s and her husband had slipped away from her when she'd made this little detour. Gripping and shaking Bridget's hands, she simply thanked the nurse for the blessed work she did. "My father would thank you himself were he still with us," she added and then with a tap on the nurse's hand she stepped away to rejoin her husband. Bridget did not get her name and did not see her again at the event.

That moment alone was enough to make her glad she had come.

She stepped deeper into the percolating and echoing buzz of the crowd and took a glass of white wine from a passing server with a *thanks*. She flowed through the little packets of guests and donors and doctors trying to make herself at least look like she belonged among them. Which is when she saw him.

Peter Edgar. *She* knew who he was. He was alone at least for the moment. It wouldn't hurt to hurry over and get a selfie with the famous bachelor, which is all she planned to do. It'd look nice on her Facebook page. She and her gang would enjoy laughing about it.

Peter Edgar slumming with the staff!

In the spirit of doing it as a lark, she approached him, said hello in a mockingly seductive voice, and asked if she could take a picture with him. He noticed her name tag with its distinctive *RN* and her department.

Peter was used to this sort of request. It happened all the time. He flagged down an older gentleman in a tux who snapped the picture of the pair of them on Bridget's phone.

She started to walk away.

"I'm Peter, by the way."

She turned her head to look over her shoulder. "Yes. I know. I've seen your plaque."

She started to walk away a second time, her phone held lightly in her hand.

"And you're Bridget?" He said it halfway between a question and a statement of fact.

"Yes. Bridget Casey. I'm a nurse in the pediatric oncology department."

Before anything more could be said by either of them, a woman came up to him and said there was someone he should meet. Bridget thanked him for the photo and turned from him and was gone. A minute later, he was joined by his date, herself a cardiologist at the hospital who'd been matched with him by a hospital administrator.

"Who was that?" she asked.

"Bridget somebody. An Irish name. She's a nurse."

"Not in my department," the doctor said.

And that exchange ended the slight connection the nurse and Peter had as they were called into dinner, where Peter and his date were at Table 2 with board members and department heads.

Bridget was at Table 12, mixed in among an oncologist and her attorney wife and a number of the lesser donors. She actually enjoyed it, helped by the free flow of wine for which she'd pay the next morning when she began her twelve-hour shift at 7.

8.

ON THE MONDAY AFTER Lenox Hill's fund-raiser, Bridget received a message from her shift supervisor. A Peter Edgar had called. Would she give him a call?

Bridget was dumbfounded. Peter Edgar wanted her to call. What could it possibly be about?

She, of course, dialed his number at her next break, still confounded by what he could possibly want.

It was simple, he told her. "How about a quiet dinner at my place?"

WTF? She knew his reputation. She'd seen him standing with the striking Dr. Walsh from Cardiology at the event. Alarm bells went off. Bridget looked nothing like the tall, gorgeous women who were regularly photographed on his arm and who, the gossips had it, usually ended up naked in his bed later in the evening. All of which only added to the, well, bizarreness of the request.

Hearing her hesitancy, he tried to explain. He was interested in seeing her but recently dragged someone into a whirl of publicity—photos and speculation—and they'd agree to end whatever they might have had with one another if it ever had had the chance to develop.

She vaguely recalled that burst of attention and remembered that she'd felt a little sorry for the girl. They'd even doxed her, and she was never heard from again. She didn't want that treatment.

Peter seemed genuinely concerned about her comfort, which is why he'd asked her to have dinner at his condo and promising to her that he wanted nothing more than dinner.

He was awkward when she arrived. The elevator opened directly into his apartment's foyer and he was waiting for her, holding a glass of expensive red wine in each hand and handing one to her as she emerged.

It took a moment for her to get a clean hold on its stem. She was stunned by the living room, something she'd only ever seen on a TV show or in a movie. *So, this is how the 1% live*, she thought.

"Welcome to my humble abode," he said with a kind smile and the hand that held the glass spread out towards the window. Humor, such as it was, was his way of calming himself for this woman who'd had an effect on him that was similar to what Amy had done, which is why he'd called her.

He'd cooked something simple and she drank more of the very good wine and while they fell easily into a pleasant conversation, it became apparent to both that there was zero romantic chemistry between them.

Still, they each had a blast, especially the way he tolerated her mocking tone, which he sometimes topped with his own self-effacement. He insisted he would pay for a car to take her home to the Bronx. In the aftermath of whatever it was between them, they both realized that it was best to keep things platonic.

Bridget was surprised, then, when as she was preparing to leave, Peter suggested that because the hospital was so close, in the future she might sleep—he made it clear that he was only thinking of *sleeping* and nothing more—in the apartment rather than schlepping to and from the northern Bronx.

"It'd be nice to have some company, friendly company, too," he admitted. The big place, he said, got lonelier more often than he liked.

It was a good offer, kindly extended, and she immediately accepted, reminding him that her dad was a cop. "And he has a gun," she added with a mockingly stern expression.

Bridget worked twelve-hour shifts, alternating between three and four days a week. Seven to seven. While it generally started at 7am and ran until 7pm, at times she'd flip it. Especially on those days when she worked the overnight, she was more than grateful to be able to walk only a few blocks to Peter's for a warm bed and a fine meal. On those overnight days, she'd always clear it the night before and Peter would usually have already headed out to work by the time she arrived.

It had become something of a luxurious second home for her, and bit-by-bit she'd personalized *her* room, which was the second largest guest room, down the hall from the master. She tried not to overstay her welcome and limited herself to showing up only when she was working two days straight and wasn't up to taking the subway home and back. It worked out for both of them.

It was a pleasant routine.

The doormen came to know her, and she had a key to the elevator. The apartment itself didn't have a key; one had to use one in the elevator for his apartment.

By the third or fourth visit, she told him that she recognized some of the paintings in the apartment. They had come with the place, he said. "I don't know anything about this stuff."

She looked at him. "You know, you really could do so much better with your money." He nodded, looking embarrassed but non-committal.

She and her mother Astrid were self-taught about art, especially eighteenth- and nineteenth-century European oils.

He sounded *interested*, which resulted in her giving him an afternoon's tour of the nearby Metropolitan Museum. It was hardly adequate for much of an education, but Bridget simply hoped it might ignite some genuine interest on Peter's part since he had the financial wherewithal to do something about it. Whether he'd used some of his money to upgrade she didn't know.

9

EVERYTHING CHANGED, THOUGH, during a particularly brutal week. The nursing staffs in virtually every department, including pediatric oncology, were cut nearly in half by a flu that rocketed through the hospital. Those able had to work every day for that week until those infected could recover, sometimes stepping in for someone newly-infected. Doctors and nurses were shoehorned into every available staff bed and the cafeteria was open 24/7.

One of those nurses was Frances Reynolds. She and Bridget had started in the department on the same day after they'd both finished their rotations among the hospital's main departments.

Frances—always Fran—lived with her mother—her father had run out years earlier—out in Astoria, Queens. She had to take the 6 Train to Bloomingdales and then switch to the N or W home. It was a twice-a-day schlep unless she took a car service with other nurses who lived in the neighborhood.

Bridget knew all this but had kept her little secret about Peter and about Peter's apartment to herself, it not being hers to share. It was greedy, yes, but she knew that Peter would be taken advantage of and his apartment would be turned into a nurses' dorm if word got out.

One early morning, though, when she and Fran came off their shift and were sitting beside one another in the female nurses' locker room, both deadly exhausted and in their scrubs, Bridget got up to make a call.

When she'd gotten back, Fran had changed into her street clothes. A much-needed shower would have to wait until she got home. Bridget looked throughout the room to confirm that they were alone. She sat Fran down beside her on a bench and leaked the news: the existence of Peter's apartment.

"You can't tell a soul," she said, "but I know someone—"

"Know?" Frances said with some skepticism.

"Just a friend, I assure you. Anyway, he has an apartment only a few blocks away with a bunch of extra rooms and I sometimes stay there between shifts."

Fran was having a hard time understanding what this relationship was between Bridget and a never-before-mentioned man who was rich enough to have a bunch of extra rooms just hanging around but that was neither here nor there given where the conversation appeared to be heading.

She let her friend continue.

"Seriously, we're just friends. Seriously."

Fran raised an eyebrow. "Sure, Jan," she said but otherwise shut up.

"Are you going to listen or just make fun of me?" Bridget asked, which caused Fran to curl her face into a mocking *I'm sorry* grimace.

After again checking to make sure they were alone, she explained that she'd just called this guy and asked if maybe she could bring a friend over since otherwise the friend would have to get herself to Astoria and he agreed.

Frances Reynolds was a lot of things but stupid was not one of them.

"So to be clear. You know this unnamed guy—"

"He has a name."

"Whatever. He's how old?"

"Late twenties, early thirties."

"Okay and this guy friend has all these rooms in an apartment and is willing to let nurses share them." Bridget nodded. "Sounds like bad porn to me."

"Seriously, Fran. I promise you he is Just. A. Friend."

Fran was flummoxed by what she was being told.

"Look," Bridget said. "I don't want this to get around but you're like my best friend here and I trust you to be discreet and so I'm asking if you want to get at least some sleep there. Nothing more than that."

"If that's all we're talking about, I'm in. But—"

"No buts. I trust him and you trust me so it'll be fine. And if it's not, I call my father."

"The one with the badge and gun?"

"I only have the one father."

Fran paused. "Okay." She assembled her things and closed her locker. "Let's go."

It was almost eight in the morning when they arrived, an hour after their brutal overnight shift had ended. Their host was waiting for them in his casual, but still expensive, work clothes. There were quick introductions but the nurses were very tired, and he hastened to head out after showing Fran to her room, leaving it to Bridget to tell her what else she needed to know.

As Peter's car took him to his office, he thought of Bridget's friend. On first impression, she was pretty, though not in a particularly conventional sense. She was about Bridget's height with dark hair that dropped a few inches below her shoulders.

As far as he could tell from their brief encounter, she was pleasantly curved. Best of all, she had a great smile and sharp eyes and he hated to admit it even to himself but his initial reaction was that he wouldn't mind spending some intimate time alone with her. If she wanted the same.

While the nurses were crashing at the apartment during the day, he got a few texts from Bridget, reporting that everything was fine and that Fran couldn't stop thanking her, and thus *him*, for what she was enjoying and it was incentive enough for him to leave a little on the early side so he could get home before they headed out to the hospital.

He made it. When he walked in, his two guests were sitting across from one another on the island of the apartment's kitchen, dressed for work and eating frozen Mexican they'd zapped in the microwave.

Peter could pay more attention to the newcomer, who'd jumped from her stool to shake his hand. She had a wonderful smile, and it pulled everything about her together. It immediately put Peter at ease.

More importantly, Peter's immediate reaction to Fran was different from what it had been with Bridget. The two nurses were similar in features, excepting Bridget's blonde hair, but even more of a spark of something that was absent with Bridget hit Peter. Much like the jolt he'd felt, figuratively and (in that case) literally, when he helped Amy Reid recover from their unfortunate meeting.

And then the two nurses were gone off to work. Peter found it peculiarly unfortunate and threw his own frozen burrito into the microwave and paired it with a fine Cabernet before sitting where Bridgit and Frances had been when he walked through his door.

After this episode was repeated the following two nights, Bridget, if she was not very much mistaken, suspected that her friend, the *guy* friend, was smitten. She liked both of them quite a bit and if anything happened between those friends, she'd be happy.

She had long since come to understand that for all the showy women with whom Peter was seen at galas and openings, he was a great romantic at heart and that part of him was afraid that his money and houses and cars were a peculiar deterrent to true love. She could imagine him as Fitzwilliam Darcy with the inherited house in East

Hampton standing in for Pemberley. She could not yet decide who might be his Elizabeth. And was she, the pediatric oncology nurse, his Bingley?

Time would tell if Fran would be *the one*, and Bridget expected it'd be interesting following along on this little drama. And if her simple act of kindness towards Fran led to something, she hoped God would reward her in the afterlife. She laughed at the absurdity of the thought.

The pair of nurses stayed overnight between shifts at the hospital several times a week even when the flu epidemic had run its course. Once this was established, Peter happily offered a plain guest room with a window facing to the west where Fran could sleep and keep some things when she wasn't heading home to spend time with her mother, Jane, in Queens.

Bridget, again being no fool and thinking herself something of a Cupid, took to excusing herself after dinner, going to her room where she could stream movies on the device Peter had arranged to be installed there (with a similar one in Fran's *de facto* space) or to the comfortable old-world library.

For their part, when Bridget was out of the way, after dinner, Peter and Fran usually sat in the entertainment room, generally fighting over what to watch on Netflix or Prime or any number of other streams Peter paid for. He usually deferred to her preferences and thus watched an inordinate number of Rom-Coms and dark and psychological subtitled Scandinavian crime thrillers. Which they'd watch on the big screen above the fireplace, sometimes to the end sometimes not from the black leather couch, which proved very comfortable for their snuggling.

It wasn't long before Fran had her own key. Soon she was staying at Peter's without Bridget. Her friend was consciously bowing out, heading home to Woodlawn after most of her shifts notwithstanding both Peter and Fran trying to have her join them.

When Bridget was not there, there was an unspoken-about but plain sexual tension at the apartment. Peter was reluctant to go out in public with Fran, after what happened with Amy Reid, but he had begun to think about it, that their relationship had grown into something of substance. There would come a time for his public acknowledgement of whatever his relationship with Fran was, he hoped, but just not yet.

To some extent, this frustrated Fran. She didn't care about being seen with *the* Peter Edgar. She simply wanted to go out with him like they were normal people. She assured him she would be okay with the gossip mill invading, but he kept telling her, *we need to give it a little more time*. He knew she didn't understand what the sudden media glare—the *Diana treatment* he called it— could do to someone who wasn't used to it.

Still, even with the informal nature of their relationship and after he explained the true nature of all of those times when he was showcased with a woman— effectively beards for his real life—she said she was fine with him continuing that bit of a charade. At least for a while. He told her that even when he went out with one of these other women, he wouldn't sleep with them as long as he and Fran were together, and the two of them fell into an increasing domesticity in their lives together.

The two were becoming lovers without realizing, or understanding, it. Fran regularly dropped her head on Peter's lap while they were watching movies, and he was blissfully content running his hand absently through her hair. His eyes lingered on her bare legs and ass when she left to go to the bathroom or the kitchen.

Fran was far from oblivious about the effect she was having on him, but after a month, she realized that Peter

45

wouldn't make the first move. It was very odd to her. He made no secret of his having gone to bed with many of his companions, some staying the night. Yet he struck her like a naïve schoolboy when it came to sex with a woman she hoped he actually cared for and cared about. A woman who was real to him.

She told Bridget this on one of the nights when Bridget was staying over. They were chomping on the Ceasar salads that had been delivered to the apartment and enjoying a chilled Chardonay while he was at some event he couldn't get out of.

"He's complicated," Bridget said. "A true romantic. Maybe you have to...well, seduce him. I can see how he wants you but I think he may be afraid if he takes one wrong step that you'll break into a million pieces or be Gone Baby Gone."

Although she had no personal experience with this sort of thing, she believed she somewhat understood Peter. Although in his case he seemed comfortable with a distinction between women-you-fuck and women-you-love, which he at least seemed to think had served him well for quite some time. It was, though, something they never spoke about.

For her part, Fran had the same sense. She'd have to make the first move. If a seductress he wanted, and *needed*, it would be a seductress he'd get.

It happened on a late Saturday afternoon, about six weeks after they'd met. It wasn't subtle.

Peter had gone into the kitchen to get dinner on. Fran started her seduction there. She followed him in, carrying a bottle of burgundy she'd uncorked in one hand and a pair of wine glasses in the other. She placed the glasses on the counter just to the right of the stove and filled both glasses about three-quarters of the way, the

46

glug-glug sound very load against the Italian-tiled walls. Glug-glug carried a certain expectation.

She held one out to him. He put his spoon down and took the glass and a long sip from it before handing it back and resuming his cooking.

Making sure he'd see what she was doing, she took a sip of *his* wine and smiled, running her tongue along the lip of his glass. She placed it down next to the bottle and her untouched glass. She slithered behind him as he resumed his onion caramelization. Or tried to. All pretense vanished when she reached around him and through the apron felt how hard he already was. *That didn't take long.*

He put the large spoon back on a plate on the stove and turned off the burner so he could rotate and kiss her properly. Before he knew or could control it, his lips hit hers with a passion he had never known, worlds different from those exchanged with his normal *guests*. His arms were around her waist as her hands pulled him closer to her lips. Her tongue invaded his mouth first, but soon his own entered hers as she relaxed her hands and ran them down his sides.

"Let's. Go. Some. Where. More. Com. For. Ta. Ble." she pleaded, using kisses as punctuation. She stepped back and untied the apron, lifting it over his head. She reached to pull his polo shirt from his slacks and off. It followed the apron to the kitchen floor. He reached for her hand and led her to the master bedroom.

The room was very large. It was on the apartment's corner, with windows facing south and windows facing west. The bed was a king-sized four-poster. The room was somewhat old-fashioned, painted in a light green, all in keeping with the place's general décor, with two armchairs on either side of a small table under the windows facing south and one could easily picture a man in a dressing gown reading there late into the night.

But there would be no reading now. Peter flung the covers aside and turned to Fran. Daylight was fading, but there was enough for them to see each other. They stood to the side of the bed. He reached for her and kissed her before unbuttoning her red blouse, pulling it from her slacks and off. He ran his hands down her sides as she stood for him until she reached around and unclasped her bra, letting it fall from her arms. It was red. And lace.

Peter gazed at Fran's tits in the near shadows, as she leaned back slightly to display them. Both his hands reached to caress them. They were, he thought, a medium-size and nice. Her skin was pale with some freckles, the areolae pink and hard. She pushed his right hand from her left tit and put her own hand below it, offering it to him. Her right hand again reached for his head, pulling it toward her left nipple, and when his lips touched it, she felt a spark. They were sensitive, and a man's mouth lightly damp always increased her arousal.

It triggered her and she dropped both her hands to the waist of his trousers awkwardly. He interrupted his suckling to step back, undoing his belt and his pants and unzipping them. He kicked off his shoes and now took off his trousers and his socks. As he was doing this, she was doing the same with her slacks, and soon each was taking in the other's body for the first time.

She was right that his clothing didn't hide faults. He was strong and thin from his gym work and running. He had solid shoulders, and his chest was only lightly muscled with no visible hair. His stomach was perfectly flat and as she looked lower she saw hair above the waistband of his briefs, which barely contained his aroused bulge.

For his part, Peter was awed by what was before him. He turned to light a small lamp on a side table and returned to take her in with his eyes. Hungry eyes, to use a cliché. Fran's tits sagged, but only slightly. She wasn't thin, but beautifully proportioned with wide hips and strong legs. He had seen many, many beautiful naked women. Some all natural. Some not.

But this, *this*, was somehow far realer to him. Perhaps it was because Peter felt a connection with Fran. It had been growing in their time together, gradually. As they had felt more and more comfortable with each other. As he regretted those nights when she hadn't stayed. As he regretted those mornings when he hadn't seen her in the kitchen or make her coffee or drink coffee she made for him in one of the T-shirts she slept in.

Now, he understood what love was. It was this beautiful, kind nurse. But he didn't have long to admire her or savor that thought as she stepped close enough to run her hand across the front of his briefs, no longer able to control his dick, its head plainly visible.

"May I?"

The question was rhetorical. Soon he'd allowed her, helped her, finish undressing him.

She stepped back, but only so she could complete her own striptease. She fully displayed herself to Peter. His tongue involuntarily licked his upper lip. She saw.

She turned to the bed and glided to it, lying at its center, onto her left side. He waited to be invited and she beckoned him with her hand before rolling onto her back. She was again displaying herself, this time more lasciviously than she perhaps ever had to anyone. She knew what he saw and she knew he wanted it. As did she.

He was soon beside her on the bed, facing her and running his left hand across her side as their eyes met and each was sure the other could hear their desperately pounding heart. With their eyes locked, she told him she was on the pill and turned on her back and he was above her and then inside her. So easily.

Inside the woman he realized he loved. He slid in completely, and he held himself till she said she was ready.

They made love.

When they'd both come, he very soon after her, he gave her a quick kiss on the lips.

"Thank you," he said happily.

"Thank *you*."

As it was getting chilly, he reached and pulled the covers over them and for the first time they slept together.

From that night on, they slept together, literally slept together and sometimes something more beforehand, whenever Fran was in the apartment. As far as Bridget could tell after Fran had revealed what they'd done, they were nearly a married couple. She still stayed over now and then because it was so close to the hospital but otherwise was content to let them discover whatever it was they were going to discover about each other.

More important, Peter and Fran felt nearly like a married couple. He cut down on the charity-dinner rounds, and speculation was rife in the papers that he had found *the one*.

Peter was trying to figure out when it was time to take Fran out and reveal her to the world as his partner. But as with telling her he loved her, he was happy to maintain the *status quo*.

With the onset of spring, they spent time at his house in East Hampton. They enjoyed the relative anonymity of a place with hordes of A-listers. Unlike before when Peter's friends joined him, he kept it private, to just himself and Fran.

10.

PETER AND FRAN FLOWED into a routine—pleasant but still a routine—when on a Thursday in early June in the apartment, Fran gave Peter the news.

She'd opened a bottle of a favorite Cabernet but poured only one glass with it. Water went into the other. She handed him the one with the wine and lifted the one with the water.

"A toast," she said, standing by one of the windows where she'd led him, "I'm pregnant."

He didn't lift his glass. He glared. It was a very cold look, and it startled and almost frightened her. She thought he would be happy. He was rich and somewhat famous and she was carrying his child.

He turned away with the glass tightly in hand and then turned abruptly back. "But I thought—?"

She took a step to close the distance he had created between them. "Peter, I screwed up. My prescription ran out and I didn't refill it. I should've told you, but, baby, we were having too much fun and I wanted it to happen."

He didn't move when she gave this explanation but his eyes tightened, harsh enough for her to recoil.

"I need to think," he finally said. He put his untouched wine on the counter, turned, grabbed his iPhone, and went to the elevator, standing and staring at its door as he waited. When he got through the lobby with barely a nod and no word to the doormen who exchanged WTF looks as he shot through and to the street, he called Bridget. She knew it was important. Calls from him had become rare.

It was early in his relationship with Fran but being the romantic soul he was, maybe he was calling to say they were engaged. She'd be happy for them.

She was blindsided when he told her about the bomb that Fran had just dropped on top of him.

"I don't know if I love her," he said as Bridget maintained her silence. He'd walked a block to the north and then to the east to avoid being seen or heard by someone from his building. "I thought I did," he continued after telling her how surprised Fran pretended to be, "but there is no way this was an accident. She's a damn nurse for God's sake."

Bridget was torn. She couldn't imagine her friend doing such a thing. *She and Fran worked together in the trenches.* But Peter was right. This wasn't an accident. She realized that she'd participated in Fran's setting up her trap, however innocent that role had been. And Peter, rich naïve Peter, had fallen right into it. It could destroy him. Not the fact of having a child—something he would be good at—but of being lied to.

Bridget couldn't say this to him. Not yet. She was in Woodlawn and told him to come up. He'd never been there but hailed a yellow cab and gave a good tip when he arrived about twenty-five minutes later. Her apartment was small but well-kempt. He dropped himself into one of her armchairs and accepted the Jameson's on ice she offered. She made one for herself.

He kept saying, looking into his swirling whiskey, that he could not understand how Fran could have done it. In a million years, he said, he'd never understand. And how nonchalant she was about the whole thing. *I thought you'd be happy.*

He looked across at his friend. "If she'd simply asked, I don't know what I would have said. Probably that it was too early but that someday I'd be ready and be ready with her, if things progressed as they were progressing.

"Then this." He spread his hands out, mimicking the explosion that nearly destroyed him then and there in his grand apartment and nearly enough to have some of the Jameson's fly out of the Waterford crystal.

Bridget reached her free hand towards his and he grasped it like the lifeline it perhaps was. She knew his instinct was to think the best of people. He did love her. At least in that way until just an hour earlier, he *had* loved Fran. But he would never commit to having a child unless he was ready to commit everything to a woman he loved and with whom he wanted to share his life. With Fran, it was too early.

After telling Bridget this in fits and starts, he quieted, sipping on the whiskey. Completely at sea about what he would do.

At about the same time, Fran was again sitting in the small living room of her mom's place. She explained the *accident* that led to her pregnancy. How unexpected Peter's reaction was to the news. How she expected that after the initial shock and surprise wore off, they would do what was right for the baby. Together.

For her part, Jane, Fran's mother, had her doubts, but her job was to avoid upsetting her daughter. So, before Fran went to her old bed in Astoria, Queens, she insisted again and again that things would work out.

11.

BRIDGET WASN'T SURE WHAT she could possibly say to Fran when they next met, as they inevitably would.

It happened only two days later. In the nurses' locker room as they were changing for their late-night shifts.

"How could you do such a thing?"

After first claiming it was an accident—Bridget said she didn't believe that for a minute—Fran admitted that she hoped he'd get her pregnant. It'd set her up for life. Even if they never married, though she'd evolved so that she very much wished she'd become Mrs. Peter Edgar, and not just for the name. She knew first-hand how tough things were for her mother, who had nothing. Not even a husband.

That fate would not happen to her.

Okay, she lied about being on the pill. It was a bonus that he was actually pretty good in bed; far better than most of her one-nighters. She had stopped doing that when her plan regarding Peter first came to her. But this growing affection for him and not his assets became a curse, a distraction to her grand scheme. It was also a blessing, though, in that this growing affection for her meant he might actually be happy and the three of them would have their fairy tale ending. Some modern-day *Cinderella*.

Bridget was taken aback by how disillusioned and untethered to reality Fran, her now former friend, had become.

Now she was brutally brought back to Planet Earth. Word would spread to every corner of the nursing staff. To her mother and her mother's close network of friends. Disownment. It was a real possibility.

All of this was circling around them both. But the immediate issue was how Fran would respond to Bridget's indictment.

"Fuck you, Bridget." Her attitude and voice had finally changed. "You're so fucking sanctimonious. I saw my chance and I took it. Okay? You were just too slow to do it yourself. I don't feel sorry for him. He's got plenty. He can give me some of it."

Bridget couldn't believe how wrong she'd been. Fran found herself with the chance of a lifetime. *We're all struggling nurses, working too hard, seeing too much.* Fran could justify it to herself. The price she paid, though, was to exile herself.

"Look around." Fran said, warming to her theme. "How many of us can you say for sure wouldn't do exactly what I did to get out of here? How many?" She flung her arms out dramatically across the locker room. "If they got the chance? I got it and I took it."

She grabbed some things and went straight into the bathroom, where she could get some peace from St. Bridget.

Even more, once she got her cash, she wouldn't have to deal with the day-to-day of being a nurse with a bunch of dying kids. A one-way ticket out of the crap she endured for years. For her and her mother. She had almost no regrets about taking it.

Bridget was shocked by Fran and her calculation. Part of it she could almost understand, the golden ticket out of Dodge. But she would never forgive her.

Bridget chose Peter.

12.

AT JUST ABOUT THE moment when Bridget and Fran were somewhat having it out at the hospital, Peter was on the phone to Evan Taylor of Enswich & Taylor. He remembered it was Amy's firm, but it had in fact been recommended to him by XTach's CEO when Peter told him that he had a personal *problem* that might create some publicity backlash.

An hour later he was wearing a path in the carpet in E&T's reception on East 40th when Evan collected him and took him to a conference room that overlooked the elaborate Art Deco building across. Much to his surprise, and a bit of embarrassment, he saw Amy Reid herself sitting at the long table with a legal pad in front of her, her cellphone lying flat to its right.

"Amy?" Peter asked, somewhat uncomfortably.

"You remember," she said with a smile as she stood.

"You know each other?" It was Evan's turn to look puzzled.

"Long story," Amy said after shaking Peter's hand and returning to her seat beside her boss. "We met on the sidewalk a while back and had coffee." She smiled at Peter and he nodded. "It didn't work out," she finished.

Evan suddenly did remember, the whole, long ago business about Peter Edgar and that photo on Page Six.

He said to Peter, "Amy spoke to me about it when it happened. Are you okay with her working on this? She's one of our best."

He again nodded, this time to Evan, and said "I'm happy to work with her."

That taken care of, the three discussed the unpleasantness that had arisen between Peter and Fran. He was embarrassed but laid it all out.

When he was done, Amy said, "Here's how I see it, Peter. You had sex with someone you had feelings for. You thought she used protection. She lied and didn't and she got pregnant. Whatever love you had for her popped. And you'll do all you can for your baby. Throw some money her way. She had no interest in marriage." She paused. "That about right?"

"Yeah."

"Peter, I'm sorry," she continued. "As far as I can tell, *you* didn't do anything wrong. Am I missing something?" He shook his head.

Evan leaned forward and asked how Peter wanted it to be handled.

After an hour or so the strategy was set. For starters, they didn't know what Fran planned to do, but it was clear that if she lied to get herself knocked up by a rich man, she wouldn't hesitate to use every social media tool as leverage to wring as much money out of him as she could.

Amy was displaying a professional ruthlessness that Peter could not have imagined she possessed during their one prior meeting. She said Fran would likely play the poor victim card, that their—and she'd make sure she always used that word—baby as a *love-child* product of the rich, entitled man's seducing her, etc., etc.

Peter interrupted. He would neither abandon nor disown the child. *His* child. He was adamant about that from the start. That's why he was meeting with Evan and Amy. To talk about how best to show the world that he would be a good father however that came about.

Evan said that E&T would do what it did best. Crisis control, in this case amounting to presenting Peter as the real victim if Fran tried to play it the other way around. He would always know that he would always cherish the product of the tawdry act that created *his* baby. Under Amy's direction, they would show that Peter had nothing to hide and nothing to be embarrassed or ashamed about.

If this made Fran the villain, so be it. That would happen, though, only if she initiated a social-media circus with its flying monkeys.

Specifically, they would go with a high-end publication to get the truth, that is, Peter's actual story, out. Evan would offer an exclusive against the backdrop of the general positive coverage he'd received so far.

Peter shook Evan's and Amy's hands after signing the formal retainer letter with its five-figure initial payment. Amy walked him to the elevator.

As they waited in the reception area where Evan had collected Peter about an hour earlier, Peter said that he was glad to have seen her again, even if under difficult if not awkward circumstances.

"It's nice seeing you, too," she replied. "I look forward to working with you on this, hard as it might be."

The elevator door opened and he stepped in. There were two people inside. As the doors began to close, he thrust his arm forward and the doors retracted. Peter jumped out, with an apology to those in the car.

"I don't know if this is appropriate," he said, "but after all that's happened would you like to have dinner with me. Something at my place so we don't have to worry about being the fodder to the gossip mills."

Since that first bizarre, long ago encounter with Peter, Amy had been keeping a closer eye on what coverage he was getting. It didn't seem that he was going out as often as he once had.

"I'll check with Evan about it, but if he okays it, that'd be nice."

"Good." He hit the elevator button again and it arrived almost immediately.

He turned when he was inside and said he looked forward to hearing from her.

She smiled, and the doors closed. She waited a moment looking at her reflection in the shiny doors. *Yes*, she thought, *that would be nice.* And she returned to her office as the elevator reached the building lobby and Peter was hailing a cab to get back to work in the Meatpacking District.

13.

WHEN PETER WAS GONE, AMY asked Evan two things. First, could she meet him outside of their work relationship? Evan said that since they met, however briefly, long before, he saw no problem with seeing him socially.

Second, could she meet this Fran? Woman to woman. With his okay, and without letting Peter know, she called the nurse, said she was with the PR firm working with Peter on the "issue," and asked if they could meet for five minutes at the Starbucks on 77th and Lex. Yes, the one where she had sat with Peter. That was coincidence; it was the closest one to Lenox Hill.

She recognized Fern in scrub-trousers when she walked in. The nurse was sitting on a stool at a tall round table by the window. Amy smiled and waved and got on line for her own coffee. She joined the woman trying to destroy, or at least wound, Peter's life. While generally introverted, Amy could be a bulldog when it came to a client.

"Thanks for meeting me. As I said I work for the PR firm that is working with Peter." She paused and took a sip of her coffee. It was very hot, and she barely drank any of it. Her next words, delivered after she'd bent down to be closer and to avoid being overheard, got the nurse's attention.

"We both know what you are. I want you to know one thing." She put her cup on the table. Fran leaned closer, curious about what she was about to hear.

It was something long and aggressive.

"We all want this to go smoothly. Peter. And you. That is, we want the story to be: we felt something for one another/we were intimate/an accident took place/it didn't work out for us as partners/we'll always be friends/the child is the most important thing/it'll be our child/I'm going to make sure he or she are taken care of."

Amy, whose voice was flat throughout and was counting on her fingers as she went, pulled herself back from the table.

"That's what I want too," Fran finally said as she tried to assess her position and feeling surprisingly intimidated by this gentle looking woman.

"Good." Amy lifted her cup. She took a longer sip of her black coffee. "I'm glad to hear it." She put her cup down and leaned forward again. "But if you get *greedy* and decide you're going to try to blackmail Peter into giving you more than the significant sum that he's willing to give you, I'm going to make sure the truth gets out. I'm in PR. I can make it happen. And if I do, when someone Googles *whore*, yours will be the first picture they see."

With that, Amy stood, grabbed her cup and lifted it in a mock salute. She walked from the stunned nurse to contemplate what she'd just been so impolitely told.

For her part and as she watched Amy maneuver her way out the store's door, Fran thought Amy was bluffing. Tearing her down would only tear the baby and Peter down with her. She couldn't be *sure* though. Amy, who she didn't yet know had met Peter in this very same Starbucks, had a steeliness that suggested she might well do what she said she would.

Fran always knew it was best not to go the love-child route. This woman confirmed her fears. She made out well enough and she would be set for life with what Peter would offer anyway. She decided to play nice and try to avoid having to have anything to do with this Amy bitch ever again. She also wanted the deal to be done as soon as possible.

The lawyers worked out the terms. Peter even paid for her attorney from a prestigious firm. That was ethical; he had no control over them.

Fran would get $3 million cash and $1 million a year for three years. A trust fund would be set up for the child. One of Peter's lawyers would be the trustee. It was contingent on confirming Peter's paternity, but Fran had no worries there; she made sure that Peter was the father and an *in vitro* test would, she knew, confirm it. Peter would have liberal visitation rights. Fran agreed to cooperate with any public-relations efforts for the child. Everyone agreed to play nice.

A month later, the piece appeared. Pictures of Peter's apartment and his house. Of Lenox Hill Hospital. Smiling shots of Peter and Fran together. The story itself was that Peter became increasingly close to Fran and they were *intimate* on several occasions. On one of those occasions, there was an *accident*. They broke up as a couple shortly thereafter, both deciding that they didn't have a future together.

When the pair learned of Fran's pregnancy, they were overjoyed, and Peter committed to ensuring that the child would be well cared for. Fran received an undisclosed payment to aid in her transition to motherhood and a trust was established for the child's benefit. Peter and Fran expected to remain *very good friends* and would share responsibility for the child's upbringing.

It was a nice story. It had just enough of the truth to be sold as believable. Amy had engineered it.

Peter had kept a low profile until the *Fran Matter* passed. Or passed as well as it could. His Wikipedia entry endured a battle between rival editors. The "man-slut" posts were promptly deleted for "poor victim" posts only to be promptly deleted by "man-slut" posts *ad infinitum*.

He didn't know this. Amy noticed it and, well, she was one of the "poor victim" editors until she recognized the futility of it and gave up.

While that whole war-of-words was petering out, Amy sat in Peter's living room. It was her first time in his apartment and they were both a little cautious about suggesting that the girl in the Starbucks photo with him was BACK!

She'd never been in a place like the palatial apartment Peter had. It took her a moment to understand the whole key-in-the-elevator set up and to have the elevator door open directly into the condo's living room. When she entered the foyer, Peter stepped up to her and handed her a glass of a very good Cabernet Sauvignon.

"It's not Starbucks but I hope it will do," he said with a smile.

She took it and enjoyed an initial sip and walked with him to the windows that faced to the west. It wasn't one of those modern high-rises with grand views across the Park and the other towering buildings that had been popping up in recent years. Instead, it was a more subdued view, the sort you'd expect from a pre-War old-world Park Avenue five bedroom.

While they stood looking out, Peter said, "Do you ever think what would have happened if that damn photo hadn't appeared in *The Post*?"

She took more of the intense Cabernet.

"Peter, frankly I didn't think of you much after that. I figured I dodged a bullet."

This was not true. It had taken her some weeks to get that fleeting connection they'd had from her system. But in this, her second chance with this man, she didn't dare admit it. She bought some time with another sip of the wine.

"I paid attention to what you were doing. Not like a stalker or anything but just because I had known someone famous. You know?"

She couldn't admit either that that brief encounter had had a powerful impact on her. How could she say that she started checking out *The Post*'s Page Six regularly and Googled him all the time? She told herself it was just keeping up to speed on an *acquaintance*, but if that's all it was, why was she comparing the men she went out with and some who she slept with to a man she barely knew and who in any case was *verboten* to her? And that the others couldn't meet the unfulfilled expectations she suddenly had.

Which is why she said what she'd said. Peter nodded, sipping from his glass. He too couldn't be honest with her. "I know."

"So," she continued, "I saw how...happy you were on your Thursday nights and the women who you walked the red carpet with."

"Now you know it was all a fake."

"Well, I suddenly saw you weren't going out so often."

"Yes. That was Fran."

She looked over at him. Her fingers lifted towards his and he let her run them across his hand.

"I'm truly sorry for how that ended."

"I know. I thought it was turning into something...special. But it didn't."

He took a deep breath and got up. "As you well know," he said, reaching his arm towards her.

"Now let me show you around the rest of the place."

The intimate moment was broken and he gave the grand tour.

When they were finished, they sat for dinner. Not at the ornate table that graced the dining room and had yet to be actually used by Peter but at the kitchen island.

Peter had ordered a cornucopia of Chinese, Japanese, and southeast Asian food, and he set the containers side by side on the counter.

"I hope I got enough," he said looking over enough to feed a baseball team.

And suddenly, in that moment with its bit of joviality, Amy felt they were again sitting naturally on stools at the Starbucks a few blocks away from Peter's expansive spread.

Their plates full and chopsticks in hand, with their wine glasses Peter had generously refilled, they sat across from each other.

After a few bites, Amy spoke seriously. "After I saw you at my office, something was triggered." She took a bite out of the dumpling dangling between her chopsticks. "What about you?"

Peter explained that he was pretty much the same. "When I saw you again in that conference room at your office, I started to wonder whether I could recapture that afternoon. Or, I guess, if *we* could."

"Me too."

They were quiet for a while. Then she asked about him. Not the Wikipedia stuff. Him.

He told her about growing up in Palo Alto. How his family was well off but truly a family. His moving east to New York and Columbia. Enjoying his job. Regularly running loops of the Park Drive in Central Park and around the Reservoir. Learning of the crash that suddenly wiped out his family, except for his Grandma Edgar.

The house in the Hamptons and the one in Belgravia.

Peter was surprised at how relaxed they now were with one another, and they agreed to another *date*, if that's what this was.

When she got home, Amy thought about it. She didn't pine for what-might-have-been. Her long-ago encounter with Peter Edgar had been upsetting. She blamed it on its suddenness and the initial shock of it. It isn't every day that you see your picture on Page Six of *The New York Post*. She thought she was over it, and she largely was.

Amy Reid was not pining for Peter Edgar. She wasn't pining for anyone. She had her job and her folks and her own brother and her small group of friends. As for love, something would come along from a man she met. It would just take time. And a bit of luck.

They were both, then, confused and excited when they had their second dinner a week later. Thai take-out delivered to Amy's place. Peter left after watching a movie on Netflix, the two of them sitting on her couch. *That* wasn't planned.

Having exhausted the not-being-seen-in-public venues, their third date was at a small burger joint on Second Avenue. They shared a booth. Amy recommended it, saying she was willing to be *seen with* him in public. Peter liked it. No one paid them any mind, apart from a few quick looks of possible Who-Dat? recognition.

Amy insisted on paying for her Caesar Salad and coffee. Peter let her.

All of this changed things between them for the good. More of Amy's time was taken up with Peter. More of her thoughts, too. The ice broken by going public together, they went to a variety of local places for dinner and strolled in the neighborhood or in the Village.

With things advancing so quickly, Peter decided that it was important for Bridget to meet Amy after making sure that Amy understood that Bridget's relationship with Peter was purely platonic. So, when the two went out, Bridget often joined them, often dragging them to the Metropolitan Museum where Bridget feared she was more lecturer than friend. In fact, both Peter and Amy enjoyed it immensely, their hands nearly always and naturally intertwined.

Peter regretted the extent to which he had cut Bridget out of his life when he was falling for Fran. It took no time for Amy to recognize that Bridget would never be a rival for the romantic love that *she* was increasingly aspiring to obtain and they quickly became very close to each other.

Inevitably, there was another piece about Peter and Amy in *The Post*. They saw it and laughed at it and then they didn't worry about it happening again.

That night, Amy called her folks. They lived in, and she'd grown up in, a center hall colonial on a dead end in Mount Vernon, the small city just to the north of the Bronx and just south of the fancy village of Bronxville. She revealed her little secret about Peter, cycling all the way back to the initial encounter on Park Avenue she had once mentioned in passing.

Her parents, Julia and Jonathan, insisted that he be brought up so they could *inspect* him. She was a dentist who practiced in the neighboring town and he a lawyer with an office in Manhattan.

And when Amy did bring her *beau* to the house, a deli spread had been set out in the screened-in porch and the four immediately felt comfortable with one another.

When Peter got up to use the bathroom, both of Amy's parents gave their seals of approval, particularly in contrast to their reactions to some of her other boyfriends about whom they were not nearly so enthusiastic.

14.

PETER PUT OFF GOING to his house in East Hampton for weeks because of whatever was brewing with Amy. It seemed too early for a weekend alone by the beach. As a result, they spent their time together in town, even hopping the subway and slaloming through the throngs of tourists as they walked across the Brooklyn Bridge to Brooklyn Heights on a Saturday when there was a slight mist.

Crossing the bridge with the multitude of little padlocks that *lovers* put there was one of those touristy things they'd never gotten around to doing in all the years they lived in New York, which made it even more fun to do.

Then, on the Saturday a couple of weeks after their stroll across the East River and three after the trip to meet-the-parents, Peter's Aston Martin pulled up to Amy's building. He called up to her—he was double parked and the City of New York doesn't care what make or model it gives $115 tickets to—and she was down in five minutes in shorts, sandals, and shades, wearing a Cure T-shirt and carrying a bag over each shoulder.

The top was down, and her overnight bag was stowed in the trunk. She put on a wide brimmed straw hat and tightened the strap that would hold it on as they headed east into the Sun.

"I feel like Grace Kelly in that Cary Grant movie on the Riviera," she said as they pulled from the curb into the northbound traffic and damn if she didn't look the part.

Within a couple of hours of their popping out of the Queens end of the Midtown Tunnel and the miles upon miles on the Long Island Expressway and smaller roads for the final stretch among increasingly exotic cars and SUVs, the two rolled into East Hampton. With the top down, it was hard to talk so little was said aloud but much was said each time he reached over to briefly grasp her hand.

After they pulled into the house's circular pebbled driveway and they were both out of the convertible, he fumbled for the keys and unlocked the door and unarmed the security system.

She was pulling her stuff from the trunk, but he took her large bag from her and they went into the foyer, where he dropped everything.

She looked across the great room to the floor-to-ceiling windows and doors that opened out over the dunes and to the expanse of the Atlantic itself.

If she thought the apartment was amazing, this was lightyears beyond that. Leaving the bags where they'd been dropped, he led her with their fingers intertwined to those windows. He swung open one of the matching doors and they stepped onto the deck, with a slight westerly wind rippling through.

The deck had four neatly arranged Adirondack chairs facing out to the ocean and a pair of beach umbrellas. Beach loungers and tables were dotted in neat clusters along either side.

But that was nothing compared to the view of the Atlantic, just over the dunes and the beach vegetation. She felt the salty spray carried by the wind and heard the rhythmic pounding of the waves hitting the beach.

Then his arm encircled her waist and she leaned her head so it was against his shoulder.

"I've been meaning to show you this for the longest time," he said, giving her waist a squeeze.

Amy was at a loss. "It is amazing." She turned. "And this, the house. I can't believe it's yours."

"It most certainly is. But while you're here, it is all yours too. Deal?"

"Deal," she said, and spontaneously she turned to face him and pulled him to her and sought out his lips and then his tongue with her own and felt a bit guilty when her thoughts drifted to what it would be like to have this wonderful kind man making love to her with the windows open and the sea breeze and sounds cresting across their naked bodies.

But this lascivious thought was interrupted when he pushed away and insisted that he still had to show her the rest. His prideful tour commenced.

After exploring all of the nooks and all of the crannies, they headed to the double doors at the eastern end of the hallway. With a theatrical *voilà*, he opened them.

The master. It was on the southeast corner. Floor-to-ceiling windows. It got the morning sun as it rose and then opened to the vastness of the ocean. He showed her the panel by the right-side of the bed that opened and closed the shades as well as the various light fixtures and ceiling fan.

The huge bed had a low and simply carved headboard in a light wood but was otherwise open. A row of pillows was against it and throws were leaning against the pillows.

The bed was covered by a down comforter in an ivory hue. It looked to be the size of a parachute.

He led her to the windows that faced to the south, holding her hand, something that had quickly become so *ordinary and natural* between them.

"Don't worry," he said. "Retractable screens have been embedded in the frames so we won't get eaten alive."

"And won't need mosquito nets."

"True. I've never imagined them as romantic as they appear in the old movies."

He tightened his grip on her hand. Oh, how the anticipation that had been growing in them both since the Aston pulled away from her curb on the Upper East Side.

"I've never been so fucking horny," he said. He paused. "Did I really say that out loud?" He looked genuinely puzzled.

She? She said nothing. Instead, she pulled him to her and then threw herself down on her back before scooting so that she lay in the plush center.

"Fuck me," she demanded. "That's all I want. For you to fuck me silly."

And she added, "And, yes, I *did* say that out loud."

There was a certain inevitability in it, for both of them. And both of them had long thought about it and were fully aware that it was going to happen when they stepped into the house.

She'd barely gotten the words out before she felt the weight of his glorious body on hers, sinking them both deeper into the bed covering.

It all fell together when she felt the taste of his lips on hers. After some maneuvering, chiefly involving discarding their clothing willy-nilly, trips to the bathroom, and the placement of a condom he'd collected from a drawer in the bureau there, they didn't just fuck. They made love. She felt Peter's arms and all the wonder of his nakedness against her own bare flesh after they'd slipped under the summer comforter and slipped into sleep of the truly loved, as she knew beyond a doubt that she was.

And a whisper he made when he thought she was asleep confirmed it and she relished in the thought and understood that whatever happened between them, she'd had at least this one afternoon she would never forget. And would always relish.

15.

PETER AND AMY BOTH knew that Amy's formal *coming out* would be a big step. They picked another hospital fund-raiser, this time in Southampton on a late-July Saturday. The objective was to introduce Amy as the *girlfriend*, the gossips be damned. They both also knew that how it was done was important as was how Amy handled it.

She was very nervous, even though Peter told her to treat it as a game, a bit of pretend.

"That's the only way a normal human being can survive. You wave. You smile. You pretend to be happy or interested or not in desperate need of taking a pee."

She laughed and realized from her own PR background that he was right. Except she'd make sure she'd pee before they got in the car.

As they drove with the Aston's top down and her styled hair protected by a Hermès scarf, he peppered her with questions.

> *Where'd you meet?*
> *Are you in love?*
> *Are you pregnant?*
> *How serious are you?*
> *What about his child?*

They had fun with it. It helped pass the time and calm her nerves.

There was no red carpet at the fund-raiser but the number of A-listers drew Paparazzi, reporters, and bloggers.

She was wearing her blue gown. The one she wore when she worked at such events. It was good enough, she

JOSEPH P. GARLAND

believed, when she was a guest at one. She bowed to that new status by wearing a pair of her wedding three-inch heels instead of the nice sling backs she wore when she worked an event.

When Peter offered to buy her a new gown, she rejected the suggestion as being premature given the newness of whatever it was that they had together.

They had had their first fight and it was about a necklace. After she buzzed him into her apartment a few days before the Southampton benefit, he'd handed her a long box from Harry Winston. She had opened it and looked back at him.

"This is too much. Way too much," she had said.

"I want you to have it."

She had lifted it from the box and ran her fingers across it. *It is too much for a date.*

"I can't accept it."

"How about if I just *lend* it to you?" he had asked when the spark of inspiration clicked in him.

So, they had resolved their first dispute. He "lent" instead of "gave" it to her for the evening. This jewelry was real and it was spectacular and more than anything she could have imagined seeing let alone wearing. Her face brightened in its luminescence, though she did not realize it.

Now, days later and a hundred mile to the east, after emerging from the British convertible and after a valet in a burgundy vest, white shirt, and bowtie opened her door, she and Peter walked in. In the event, she easily handled the questions lobbed at her from the gauntlet of reporters behind a line of metal barricades and under the watchful eye of Southampton's finest.

Once inside, they were both pleased with how things had gone and she was fascinated by having been on the other side for a change.

She'd get used to it. If, that is, the world of being with the Peter Edgar became real.

16.

THINGS HAPPENED QUICKLY AFTER that. Peter, it turned out, was himself fairly clever. After the whole ado about Amy and their stepping forward to control at least some of the narrative about the charmed life of the Peter Edgar, he increased his dedication to his work at XTach. Unlike his father, sales were not his strength. Nor were the complicated financial scenarios that his brother had handled with seeming ease. He, instead, was a natural strategist. A *big picture guy*.

As his father had combined his financial and marketing skills with his Stanford friends' technical expertise, with his inherited boatload of money, Peter decided to take a stab at creating something in cooperation with XTach. He spoke to his boss, the one who'd led him to the NYPD detective that told him of the loss of his family that early evening a few years before. He pitched his idea, and his boss signed off on it.

With that endorsement, Peter invited several engineers at the firm for dinner in a quiet, private room a few blocks from the office. He made it clear from the outset that if they came up with something that had some promise, he'd be the initial moneyman but he would give credit where credit was due. He was putting in the seed money but they'd each get a small equity stake.

He named it MCE Global after his parents, Michael and Carly Edgar. It would be an incubator for ideas. Its existence, in turn, enticed talent to come to XTach. The eternal cycle in Silicon Valley and similar places around the globe implanted in Manhattan's somewhat pretentiously named *Silicon Alley*.

It was a while later, but he formally left XTach to focus on that incubation work. It would be a while as well until he knew which of those ideas would work. He could wait. And he'd given his former company a right-of-first-refusal of anything that came out of it.

As for Amy, they met several times a week for dinner, sometimes at restaurants and sometimes at the Park Avenue condo. She usually stayed over and while she had a guest room that was informally assigned to her, she rarely used it; the bed in the master was more than large enough for the two of them—Peter sometimes thought it might be too large, that when he woke in the night she seemed far too distant (physically) than either of them liked, particularly given their penchant for sleeping against one another.

For her part, Bridget often stayed over when she was working back-to-back days but always deferring to Peter and Amy. She rarely joined them when they went to the house but it was always magical to the two new lovers, the memory of their *first time* pleasantly melded into each of them. Amy and Peter felt free to go out in public, becoming just yet another couple among many who were far richer and unlike them preternaturally prone to scandal in an oasis of people who strangers similarly recognized.

Things were even less visible after Labor Day in the Hamptons and after the annual retreat west by the short-termers like birds migrating south at the outset of winter.

Which explains why that beach at the bottom of the staircase from Peter's deck was almost deserted in mid-September. Peter and Amy went down before dinner. They were nearly alone in that particular sound of the ocean beach and the voices echoing off the water.

The two were walking west, towards the setting sun, each in shorts, sandals, sunglasses, and T-shirts. They each wore a wide-brimmed hat that Amy had insisted be part of the house's fashion code, hats like Australian cricket players wear in the midday sun.

They were some feet to the side of the water line away from where the waves died out. They had left their sandals on the bottom step of those stairs and the sand was soft and mingled between their toes and across the soles of their feet. Their hands were clasped together and their arms moved like a contented pendulum, in perfect rhythm with their steps.

Feigning nonchalance, Peter asked Amy to move in with him. Here and on Park Avenue.

"I don't know, Peter," she answered without looking at him and to his surprise. "I'm pretty settled in my own place." Which would fit in Peter's kitchen. Almost.

He abruptly stopped and they turned to face each other. He held his hand above his eyes to block the sun. The wind had come up, and beads of mist hit them from the ocean. He was so sure that everything was going swimmingly.

She was genuinely guilty about his reaction. She reached her hand to his.

"You could always sweeten the deal."

He was further surprised. She thought how naïve he still was even after the business with Fran.

"Are you negotiating?" he asked, with a twinge of umbrage.

"No," she said with the evil smile he'd come to appreciate as an intimacy between them. She had actually internally rehearsed this very scene and everything was going according to plan.

"I have a reputation and it would be tarnished should I become your...kept woman."

He stared at her and her broad smile. The wind had picked up even more and her hair was being sprayed hither and yon and they were being sprinkled with droplets from the Atlantic.

"You," he started. "You mean you don't want to just move in. You want to…marry me."

"Only if you, you know, ask."

The haze that had enveloped him like Darcy's reaction to Elizabeth's initial rejection, slipped away and he smiled.

"I wasn't sure what you'd say," he said.

"Only one way to find out."

"But I don't have—" he said, feeling lost, patting his empty pockets.

"Peter. If you know anything about me it's that I don't care about frivolous things, no matter how expensive." There was no denying the monetary reality but she did her best to cast it aside.

"A kiss from you will seal the deal," she offered.

He leaned closer to her so he could have his lips touch hers.

She pulled her head away. "But you still have to ask."

A moment of confusion hit him but he was quickly over it. Instead, he lowered himself so he had one knee on the sand in front of her. Several of those who were near them on the beach stopped to watch whatever was unfolding unfold.

Amy extended her left hand and he took it very, very gently.

"Will you marry me?" he asked.

She put her hands on his shoulder as a signal for him to get up. When he had, she wrapped her arms around his neck.

"Of course I will," she began and then pulled back slightly so they could seal the deal with a kiss.

She looked at him and ran the side of her wrist beneath her nose to clear away a tear that had escaped. She said through a grand smile, "Oh, my darling. You can be such a fool. But at least you'll be my fool."

They held each other as tightly as they could and kissed properly, all while being coated with the Atlantic Ocean's mist and in the gaze of the assembled strangers who were witnessing and in some cases filming the couple's moment of pure bliss.

Peter's generally inactive Facebook page carried the announcement. Apparently people followed it; an item about it appeared on Monday's Page Six, *The Times* mentioned it on its Society page, and it promptly appeared on Wikipedia:

> *Speculation about his intentions with Amy Reid ended when they agreed to get married on a beach in East Hampton. Wedding date and location as yet unknown. She was the woman who was outed a few years back as a possible love interest for Edgar, before she suddenly disappeared. Apparently her absence made his heart grow fonder and now she is indeed the one.*

It was not entirely smooth sailing, though. They fought about a prenup. *She* insisted he have one. *He* insisted that they not. They compromised. If they divorced, she would get $100 million as long as the marriage lasted more than twenty-four hours from the *I dos*.

They signed it in his lawyer's office.

17

FOR SOME REASON, AFTER he'd become engaged, Peter became concerned about how Fran would treat the child. There was nothing to suggest anything or that Fran wouldn't be a good mother, but Peter uncharacteristically became convinced that some type of intervention was in order. Amy agreed with him.

For her part, Bridget thought it was inappropriate and dangerous but she was outvoted. She agreed to be there, though, as a buffer between the two-on-one confrontation she was afraid would happen.

Peter had seen Fran about once or twice a month since the deal was signed and the money was transferred.

Initially, these visits were to the apartment in Astoria that Fran shared with her mother. With her enhanced bank account, though, Fran decided she deserved something far, far larger and more prestigious.

She found a broker in one of Westchester's toniest and most elite suburbs and did a tour of house after house until she found the perfect one. She had her mother come up to see it. Jane thought it was a bit isolated but Fran brushed that concern off. So, she bought it.

It was a five-bedroom, 5,231 sq. ft., newly-built house on a two-acre lot on a dead-end—"*cul de sac*" at these prices—in affluent Purchase, New York.

She'd gotten a blue Lexus SUV immediately after Peter's first payment cleared and had kept it garaged in Queens. Now with a three-car garage and a circular driveway, the least she could do was to add something flashier, more Westchester elite, which in her case turned out to be a sleek red Mercedes coupe.

Every few weeks, Peter would drive north in his Aston to spend some awkward time with the soon-to-be mother of his child, who they now knew would be a girl. But he never stayed long, especially when Fran's mother Jane was with them.

As the due date neared, Peter had asked Fran to stop by at his apartment the next time she was in the city. That ended up being about three weeks after the offer.

On that night, Fran was very big. When she stepped out of the familiar elevator for the first time since her blowup with Peter, three people were positioned around the living room, each trying to look nonchalant. Fran was surprised about the third one. Bridget. She didn't know that Peter had pressed her to be with them, acting as something of a buffer or mediator for whatever might happen. She realized too late that she should have insisted on a neutral location.

Peter scurried over to see if Fran needed help. He offered her a non-alcoholic drink. She said she was happy with water.

With some effort, they all finally settled *very* uncomfortably, with Fran in a chair for support, Peter and Amy on the sofa, and Bridget on the chair that matched Fran's, but was not too close. Fran said to her erstwhile friend Bridget, "I didn't know you'd be here."

"Peter thought it might help to have a friend's face," she answered.

"Former friend," Fran said dismissively and consciously turned her attention in Amy's direction. She was surprised at how friendly Amy at least pretended to be. Amy'd even given the visitor what might have been a well-meaning hug when she'd come into the apartment.

Fran didn't really fall for it. This was, she'd understood from the moment Peter had suggested the visit, all about boosting his connection with Fran's daughter. His daughter.

Her job in this three-on-one negotiation was to give away as little as possible, particularly in the area of ultimate control over the baby, while maximizing what she got in exchange. She remembered that she had to be careful with that soon-to-be wife of his, the one who nearly put a knife to her throat at the nearby Starbucks not long before. But she'd come out of that first negotiation pretty well under all the circumstances and expected she could do pretty well this time too.

The calm didn't last long. To the shock and dismay of everyone, as the efforts at small talk floundered into empty space, Amy let emotion get the better of her. She knew she shouldn't. But she did. She leaned closer towards Fran. Fran thought she was trying to smooth things with the group.

Amy's voice low, she said, "I'll be straight with you. If I never ran into you again, I'd be happy. But that's not going to happen because of the baby. I promise that I will do whatever I can in the baby's interest. You had better do the same. If you do, I can, and Peter can, move forward. I'll just leave it at that. I'm giving you a chance to redeem yourself."

This unnerved Fran. Not just the threatening words but the suggestion that Fran would do anything to betray her child. Peter's fiancée was threatening her again and she wasn't even bothering to sweettalk it. This was an ambush.

She stood, knocking over the half-empty glass of water she'd placed on the coffee table when she sat and the water dribbled onto the expensive rug. Her voice rose. "This is my child and I will take care of her. I've agreed to the terms Peter insisted on for visitation and what-not. I'm not going to have either of you second-guess how I raise my child. MY DAUGHTER."

The last words were said slowly and precisely and while they were still echoing through the shocked room, Fran was up and grabbing her things from the table by the elevator door where Peter had placed them. She rang for the elevator while the others remained frozen in the plushness of a wealthy family's Park Avenue condominium.

Long after she was gone, the others still had not moved. Peter and Bridget, stunned and confused, turned to Amy. She was reddening. She knew the moment the words had left her mouth that she was fucking everything up. The calm détente Peter had so carefully built was gone.

"I don't know why I did it," she said. "I have no excuse. It was the anger that built up about what Fran did to Peter, how *evil* it was. *She* was. Without thinking I wanted to know that Peter would not let her walk all over him with their child. That we'd do what we thought best to protect the little girl."

Peter was never again as angry at Amy as he was at that moment. It was fortunate that Bridget was there.

"I've worked so hard—" he began, leaning into his hands in front of him.

The two women heard in his voice what he had gone through for his child. "I just can't believe what you said."

At that, Peter turned to storm out of his own apartment. Amy and Bridget were shaken and quiet, watching helplessly as he waited for the elevator.

When he was gone, Amy said, in tearful spurts, "I just wanted to make her understand that we'd take care of the baby if she didn't."

Bridget said she got it but that she also understood where Fran was coming from. For all her lying and deception, Fran would never do anything other than what she thought was best for her child. Even though it was Peter's as well, she was a mama bear and would not let anyone challenge that status.

Bridget had gradually softened over time in her view towards her one-time friend and colleague, if only because of the baby. She would talk to Peter to see if there was any bridge she could help build or rebuild. For now, though, she simply kissed Amy on the forehead and told her to be there when Peter returned. And she left.

It was late when Peter came home. Amy was sitting on the sofa in the dark living room. Since Bridget had herself disappeared down the elevator as Fran and then Peter had done minutes before, Amy'd moved only once, to go to the bathroom and get a glass of water. She didn't get up when he stepped off the elevator. He sat beside her on the sofa and reached for her hand, which she reluctantly allowed him to take. It was chilled and he placed his other hand atop it and rubbed.

At the touch, she began to slightly chortle. She managed to get enough control of herself to try to apologize but he interrupted her. He leaned over and kissed a tear that had begun drifting down her right cheek. He reached for her other arm and turned her so they faced each other, though he had to lift her chin so he could gaze into her damp eyes.

"Ames. I know you did what you thought was right. For me. For the baby. I only wish you'd spoken to me about it ahead of time. What's done is done. We can get through this." After he ran his fingers across her cheek, he said, "I love you."

"I'm so sorry Peter. I love you so much. I didn't know I was going to do that and once I started I couldn't stop even though I knew it was wrong while I was doing it. I'm so sorry."

She was shaking slightly, on the verge of losing control. He leaned in and kissed her forehead. "I know, I know," and those words and that kiss were like the bursting of a dam and her tears came and she shook while he held her, lightly circling her upper back with his hand, and he tightened his hold.

After she'd showered, she felt more like herself and not the evil, vindictive bitch that was on display when Fran had sat down opposite her. They struggled through dinner together. Amy still had her apartment nearby. She offered to leave, but he asked her to stay. He wouldn't hear of her going. They went to bed early. Both pretending to be asleep until each eventually was.

It took days for the two to get back in sync. Peter knew Amy was thinking of him when she'd spoken to Fran in the way that she had. Amy knew she'd fucked up. It took them a few days before they spoke about it again, and when they did they both realized that the issues she'd raised with Fran would probably have arisen anyway. Amy's mistake was vocalizing them in a situation that Peter was trying to use for some sort of reconciliation for the baby's sake. He knew about Amy's prior meeting with Fran at the Starbucks and although he wasn't entirely pleased about that either, he understood that then, too, she had his interests at heart. Things turned out well after that and they hoped the same would happen with this incident.

And it did. Peter was able to get Fran to be cooperative again. She made it clear that she never wanted to see *that bitch* again. When he told Amy that, his fiancée simply said, "that makes two of us."

18.

THE WEDDING OF AMY REID and Peter Edgar was a modest affair. No formal announcement appeared ahead of time. Not a single Insta post detailed the simple but uber-elegant floral arrangements that filled the East Hampton house where the ceremony and reception would take place. No photographer sat for hours on end awaiting the arrival of guests to capture their couture gowns.

It was just how the bride and groom wanted it. A chilly November Saturday, the one before Thanksgiving. It was held in the great room of the East Hampton house. The weather was very cold but at least the sky was blue with traces of clouds drifting overhead which meant that there was no rain. But the chill put the kibosh on the possibility of having the ceremony on the deck.

The guests filled the rooms in the house and stayed at nearby places that Peter had booked. Amy's folks, her brother, and her mom's parents—her dad's were dead—Bridget, several people from Enswich & Taylor, including Sarah and Evan, several from MCE Global and XTach, and five or six other friends of the bride or groom. All were transported to the south fork of Long Island in a fleet of black Escalades that Peter had arranged as transport. For those who could play hooky on Friday, their rides brought them out on Thursday night so they could enjoy an extra day in town and they and the others were picked up one by one in Manhattan or Brooklyn before arriving.

Peter arranged for Grandma Edgar to be brought from the facility in nearby Bridgehampton, and he led her into the house and to a chair of honor among those placed on the floor.

Amy's mother had argued for a Catholic Church ceremony, but Amy's agnosticism and Peter's lapsed Episcopalianism defeated that suggestion. Fran and Jane were invited, but they RSVPed NO—Fran was eight months along.

The house was moderately decorated with stirrings of white ribbons dangling along the wide staircase and white roses were set in vases spaced liberally around the great room. Beyond the makeshift wedding archway was the Atlantic, its wave caps reflecting the sparkling sun.

Beyond the flowers and streamers, several photos were placed on a cabinet along part of the room's left wall. Most prominent among them was one taken at this very house, on the deck that was too cold for the ceremony.

It was of the four Edgars, taken during that last summer they had together. In that small yet meaningful momento, Peter had those family members with him. They would have liked Amy.

Bridget was the maid of honor, and she walked down the stairs in a dark maroon silk dress that matched what Amy would soon reveal was her own. Both were custom made by a seamstress and her team at a loft in Cobble Hill, Brooklyn. Bridget carried a posey of small maroon roses and was met with Peter's best man, Eric from MCE, at the bottom and they stepped arm-in-arm to the makeshift archway. When they were in place, a string quartet switched from Mozart to the opening bars of *Here Comes the Bride*, one of Amy's concessions to her mother that everyone agreed to in the festive spirit that had overtaken the happy band of celebrants, Amy floated carefully down the stairs like a sort of starlet in a white dress from the same Brooklyn atelier. It was not quite a gown but fit the aesthetic wonderfully. She carried herself more nervously than anyone, especially her, expected and tightly gripped a bouquet of white roses that matched the ones spread about the room.

On her left wrist was a beyond dazzling diamond bracelet that would have blinded the room with its reflections had Amy been a step or two closer to the array of windows. It had been custom-made for Peter's mother and gifted to her by his father on their twentieth anniversary. Its clasp had his mother's initials CE engraved. Amy insisted that they remain and before she had started down the stairs she had rubbed a finger across those initials and for a moment her happiness was undermined for the absence of a woman she would never meet but whose life had been so important for her future husband.

She had choked away that tear just as the opening strains of the Wagner piece crested through the large room.

The bracelet was something old. A pair of her mother Julia's diamond stud earrings, themselves a gift from her father to her mother for *their* twentieth, was her something borrowed.

Dangling over her left garter was a long one-inch-wide strip cut from the hem of the gown she'd worn at her coming out with Peter at that Southampton gala. It was her something blue.

And the something new? It was silk and bespoke. And invisible to the guests. Bridget? She was wearing an identical lingerie ensemble. In the maroon of her dress.

Jonathan, Amy's dad, was waiting for her at the bottom of the broad wooden staircase. He led her to Peter, himself wearing a simple, traditional tuxedo as was his best man.

After a kiss, Jonathan handed the bride to the groom and stepped to the side, next to Amy's mother.

The ceremony itself was short, consisting of simple vows written by the couple themselves. The bands were simple too. They matched each other and matched the pair that were worn by Peter's parents on the day they died.

The caterers quickly swapped the rows of chairs for round tables, smaller than ones normally seen at a wedding so they would be more intimate.

The couple obliged those who insisted on them having at least one dance as husband-and-wife, and they held each other close to the quartet's rendition of the slow movement of a Mozart quarter piece. And though the space that had been created for this was small, they were joined by several other couples, particularly Amy's parents, as that slow movement faded and the next, faster one took over.

After yet another formality that Amy's mom proposed, the cutting of a cake baked at the couple's favorite East Hampton bakery, it was time for them at least to head out.

A car was waiting for them. It was late so they couldn't take a pretentious Hamptons helicopter. Instead, they were whisked along the now quiet highways that led them to JFK and from there they flew first class to Heathrow and at around noon local time, less than twenty-four hours after they'd become Mr. and Mrs., they were greeted by a hired staff at Peter's house in Belgravia for their honeymoon.

There was a small announcement in *The Sunday Times*'s Weddings page and an edited Wikipedia page.

19.

ON A MID-DECEMBER EVENING, the Edgars were just back from London when Peter received a call. It was from Jane, Fran's mother. Fran was in labor. She was having the baby in White Plains, not too far north of the city. Peter and Amy took a car up and sat with Jane.

Fran was still in labor. As had been arranged, Peter and Jane joined her in the delivery room. Several hours later, the daughter was born. 7 lbs., 10 oz. After Fran cuddled with her, she passed the little one to her father. After this first intimacy, Peter passed the little one to the new grandmother. Amy sat alone in the waiting room.

Fran exercised her prerogative to name her.

Eve Petra Reynolds

Two months after Eve's birth, Amy drove the Aston up to Fran's house in Purchase. She'd called ahead and after initial reluctance, Fran said she'd listen to whatever Amy had to say. No promises.

At the large, isolated house with tinges of snow surrounding the base of the shrubbery along its front, Amy stood for a moment before pushing the bell. Fran had seen the car pull into the circular drive and herself paused a moment to prepare her face before opening the door. The two exchanged the slightest of greetings, amounting to little more than nods and *Fran* and *Amy* as the case required.

Fran led Amy into the vast, sterile living room. It was clear that this nearly blindingly white room was perhaps the least visited part of the house. It was a place to impress, not to live, but Fran was trying to impress her guest and so that's where they went.

Amy agreed to Fran's offer for coffee and the host directed a servant to bring out a tray. While they waited, they exchanged small talk about married life (for Amy) and life in the suburbs (for Fran).

"I went to college not far from here," Amy said and Fran could do no more than a flat, "Yes, I've been told."

They were saved by the arrival of the coffee and a plate with some Digestive biscuits. Things, such as they were, paused while the maid poured the coffee and Fran added some milk and put in two teaspoons of sugar. Amy took hers black.

They each lifted their cups and saucers and took a sip before restoring them to the table, a sign that the preliminaries were concluded.

Amy spoke first. She admitted she had been way out of line. In fact, it was a different Amy from the one who Fran had met twice before. Those times, Amy was protecting Peter. He no longer needed protection. She promised Fran that she would never presume as to what Fran did with Eve.

"Peter is the most important thing in the world to me. Eve is a close second. But I'm not her mother. If you need anything, let me know. We can keep things just between us."

Fran was suspicious. She wouldn't tolerate any second-guessing. Not from Peter. Not from Amy. She took Amy's number and half-heartedly thanked her for coming.

They'd never be friends. Both knew and accepted that. But Fran agreed that Amy could be in the room when Peter came to visit Eve. Maybe they could tolerate one another for that at least. For Eve's sake if for nothing else.

20.

THINGS CALMED DOWN WITH the new year. The newlyweds had Christmas at their apartment. Amy's folks and grandparents, Bridget and her parents and grandparents. Eric, the best man from DCE Global, and three or four XTach programmers from out of town, including one from Mumbai, and a Lenox Hill nurse from County Kerry in Ireland joined them.

Fran and Jane were invited as a gesture but they couldn't come, including because Eve wasn't yet two weeks old. Peter arranged for a catered dinner to be delivered to Fran's big house in Purchase. Plus Eve got fancy baby paraphernalia. For the others, Peter sent a sapphire necklace for Fran and a pair of diamond stud earrings for Jane.

On the first Sunday in January, Peter ran two laps of Central Park. Twelve miles. It was cold and he wore tights and a long-sleeve shirt with a hat and gloves. Amy would have breakfast ready when he got home, which gave him the incentive to push the final miles, finishing atop the famous Cat Hill on the east side of the Park and near the Met Museum.

As he jogged to the apartment and the omelet that Amy promised him, his mind drifted back. Eighteen months earlier, he was very rich and very famous and not much else. Now, his wealth and fame were the least important things about him. To him. Sure, he wasn't about to give them up, especially the money part, but they no longer defined him. He had a wife and a child. Some dear friends. He was excited at his job every day. He'd become passionate about his running and joined one of the city's more serious running clubs.

As he headed east, crossing the avenues and streets that would get him home, he was the picture of contentment. As always, he passed over the spot where he had walked, literally, into Amy. He smiled as he did, as always.

After he greeted the doormen, he was supremely content as he rode the elevator up. His wife, alerted from the lobby, held a glass of water and a cup of coffee for him as he stepped into the condo before heading off for his shower, hoping that Amy might defer breaking eggs for his omelet so she could...*wash his back.*

21.

THE GROWING HAPPINESS of the family was disrupted by the passing of Grandma. He visited her, usually with Amy and sometimes with Bridget, when they were at the house in East Hampton. While her mind remained clear until near the end, her ninety-year-old body could not keep pace.

This was evident early in the new year. She'd been too fragile to move for Christmas, and Peter and Amy had driven over on Boxing Day to be with her. She was in a contemplative mood and shared stories with Amy of the in-laws Peter's bride would never know. Amy had heard most of them before, some many times before, but she loved slipping into Peter's old, long-gone world and the reminder that she would never meet Peter's folks or his brother again tugged at her heart.

Then, just past her ninety-first birthday, Grandma Edgar's deterioration was clear. Peter and Amy both arranged to work from the house and Peter spent several afternoons each day at the facility. Until she was barely conscious and was taken by ambulance to a hospice facility in Westhampton Beach. Three days later, with Peter and Amy in her room, she slipped away and for a while Peter was the last Edgar standing.

22.

FOR EVE'S SIX-MONTH birthday in June, Peter invited Fran, Eve, and Jane—Eve's grandmother—to East Hampton. It would be the first time Peter saw his daughter outside the hospital or Fran's house. Amy's trip to Fran and her genuine apology had, it was hoped, cleared the air so that they could all get along, at least in the interest of the baby girl.

It was not long after the three Reynoldses arrived that everyone assembled on the deck in the late afternoon with beer and wine, bowls of chips and salsa spread around. After having thought about it for a very long time, Fran asked Amy if she'd like to hold Eve. Amy was desperately hoping that Fran would extend this offer, and when she did she agreed. Eve was passed from one woman to the other like the most precious of cargoes, which, of course, in many ways she was.

Amy held the baby briefly and made funny faces at her before Fran asked Bridget if she wanted a chance, which she did and the ritual of cuddling with the infant was complete.

Amy was deeply and unexpectedly affected by the exercise, though not so anyone would notice. It was as if the decision had been made for her. The tangibility of a new creature. It hit her.

I will carry Peter's child.

When they had the place alone to themselves, she would tell him.

After a dinner prepared by many amateur cooks and with the beach virtually empty, the group climbed down the thirty steps to the beach and strolled along the water. Eve was sleeping in a snuggly worn by Peter, walking between Amy and Fran. Bridget and Jane spoke quietly and vaguely some steps behind them. After ten or fifteen minutes, the group turned back. When they were inside or on the deck, everyone made themselves at home.

Tensions eased even more when the group lounged around the next day. They went to Bridgehampton, a town over, for lunch and another stroll. It was Sunday, though, and Jane had to be at work in the morning so soon after Eve crashed, they loaded Fran's red Mercedes and after an exchange of mutual hugs, the visitors were off to Westchester.

After a quick dinner, Peter himself left in an Uber, leaving Amy and Bridget alone for their week-long vacation. Peter would come back in a few days.

The two women, now the best of friends, lounged on the deck on Sunday night after sunset and after getting their feet sandy in a fifteen-minute stroll through the few remaining visitors to the beach, with the eerie sounds of an ocean beach at dusk.

Each had a glass of wine. The only sounds were the waves lapping against the sand and the occasional voice being carried through the still air. That first family weekend was over and the consensus was that it had gone better than anyone expected.

Sitting in an Adirondack chair next to Bridget in hers, Amy turned noticeably and unusually quiet. Bridget recognized how her friend had reacted to Eve and gave her room to process things.

Peter was gone for only a few days and was back on Thursday. When he was, Amy drove Bridget into town to catch the Jitney bus back to town to pick up some things and to give them some time together.

It felt strange to both Amy and Peter to simply be alone together at their house. Recently, there were usually others with them. When it was just them again, though, they remembered how much pleasure this simple thing of being alone gave them. As the sun was setting, they sat on the deck. After an extended silence Amy said, "I want a baby." She paused. "I want *your* baby."

Peter wasn't entirely surprised. He may not have been the most observant of creatures, but even he noticed how Amy had reacted when she held Eve. He reached over for his wife's hand. He simply said, "Let's make it so."

Their hands touched and they exchanged *I love you*s. She got up. As she headed into the house, she called to him, "how about now?"

He followed her to the master, chasing her giggling body up the wide staircase. They kissed as they stood next to the bed, amid more *I love you*s.

"Let's make a baby."

They ran hand-in-hand up to the wonderful bed where they'd made love—and sometimes fucked—countless times. This one was different. He lowered himself and she guided him into her. This would be the first time it was done without a condom. It felt magical, more than ever, with each of his thrusts.

And when they were done and they lay on their backs beside each other and their fingers intertwined, each wondered whether they had just entered a new world from which they could never return. Amy cried, but so lightly that Peter didn't even realize it.

Still lying together, Amy heard snoring. Peter was asleep, his right foot flat on the sheet so his knee was in the air. She reached her hand to her stomach. Holding it there, she did something she hadn't done for decades. She prayed. She didn't know if she believed in god, or at least the god she was exposed to growing up, but for this she wasn't taking chances. She prayed.

The baby-thing put their subsequent lovemaking into a whole new light. It interjected a spontaneity that neither dared experience before. Now all-bets-were-off and they were like randy lovers, always ready to make love or fuck or do any number of things in between when alone. Bridget noticed the difference and when she saw The *Look* in one or the other's eyes, she found something to keep her occupied elsewhere in the house or the condo.

Amy's prayers were answered. At least in theory. Shortly after she missed her next period, a test confirmed it.

They told one person. Bridget.

23.

IT WAS AMY'S IDEA. Shortly after the weekend in East Hampton where Eve was passed around and everyone fell in love with her, and after she and Peter hoped they'd created their own child, Amy suggested that Peter might find some useful things to do with some of his money.

The Peter and Amy Edgar Foundation was the result.

There was only one person that they thought could be its director. When Peter asked her, though, Bridget said she didn't want the job. It was something in which she had no experience and taking it on would mean she'd have to give up being a practicing nurse. But when Amy joined her husband with regard to the request, she relented.

After poaching talent from a few other New York non-profits, Bridget Casey was formally named the executive director of the Foundation, with an office in Rockefeller Center. The Foundation's purpose was to make grants to small firms and institutions doing pediatric-oncology research. It would act something like Peter's own incubator fund, seeking to finance promising firms in the child cancer business.

Bridget's years as a children's cancer nurse eased her transition. Plus, it became clear very early on that she was very good at her new job.

24.

FRAN, TOO, WAS AFFECTED by that weekend at the Hamptons house. She was surprised when she realized how much she had actually *enjoyed* being there. So distinct from the loneliness that had encompassed her since she cut the deal with Peter and was cast out from the entirety of her prior world, even in some ways by her own mother. Not to mention her physical isolation in a tony Westchester suburb.

And there she was. It wasn't just the house. It was the life. The people. Sure, there was more than a little resentment towards her, but Eve had provided a bridge and even bitchy Amy had softened after she'd held the small girl. The contrast to her supposed luxurious life at her own home ate at her.

Now with Eve in that grand house, she still hadn't met her neighbors. At best she'd see one older woman walking her chocolate lab and bending down to pick up after him and a creepy-looking guy who'd hurried along with his golden retriever each morning. Even when she took Eve out in the stroller, no one bothered to speak to her, the only people in sight the guys mowing lawns and trimming hedges. The FedEx and UPS drivers.

Fran spent time in the sculpture garden of a nearby corporate headquarters and in the high-end mall in White Plains a few miles away. Still, the only people who spoke to her were salesclerks, the maids who came to the house twice a week, Eve's nanny, and those inquiring about Eve.

She took comfort in her ever-expanding stock of sex toys. The toys and porn were her sole respite from her time—which she loved more than anything—with Eve. Even with the crying or sick Eve.

Fran had gotten back on the pill. She sought to renew old friendships. Male friendships. Some, even some now-married ones, were receptive although it never got past empty, flirtatious sexting. Except with one single-but-engaged oncologist who lived a few towns over. On two or three Saturdays, she booked a room at a luxurious hotel in White Plains and they fucked. Then he got a case of the guilts and word must have gotten around because suddenly no other MDs were receptive to any form of communication with her anymore.

After that disaster with the cancer doc, Fran was shaken when she realized that she was thinking more and more of Peter while she was doing herself. At times she would even say his name to get her over the hump to her orgasm.

This realization made her very uncomfortable but there was no one she could talk to about it. If she had a friend to confide in, her own Bridget, she might have. But she didn't. Which was the impetus for her to head up to Greenwich for some twice-a-week therapy sessions with a shrink.

At home, she was also having coping issues. She had those maids who kept to their duties quietly and a nanny to watch Eve so she could get out of her self-imposed prison.

Which is why Jane was taken aback when Fran called her one night and said she needed help with Eve. Fran had no job and nothing but time, yet she couldn't raise her own child alone?

Jane had been a single mom with nothing but a sister who stayed at home with her own kid back in Astoria while she went to work and somehow managed to raise Fran to become a registered nurse.

But Fran? Boatloads of money and help and she needed her own mother to step in to *help*?

Jane had tired of Fran's demands and cut down her trips to Purchase to every other week, using an Uber that Peter insisted she take. This had the effect of creating even more resentment and self-pity for her daughter, but Jane had had enough.

Which is how things stood when about four months after everyone's trip out to East Hampton with Eve and Jane, the week before Thanksgiving, Jane received a call from her daughter.

"Mom. I need you. I've been arrested."

It was a little after three in the afternoon. Fran had been driving home from White Plains when she took a turn a little faster than she should have. The Mercedes slid into a pole on one side of an array from which several traffic lights dangled. She was okay and thank God Eve wasn't in the car.

Fran had just spent almost two hours getting herself soused. As shown by a roadside sobriety test and a follow-up at the White Plains Police Station.

After wandering aimlessly around that city's high-end mall, she had decided to get lunch in town and ended up at a pub on Mamaroneck Avenue. She wasn't very hungry, but the first glass of a chilled wine went down well and the second even better. The restaurant was dark, the type of place she imagined was for illicit liaisons or money drops.

She sat alone at a table near the bar. Businesspeople coming and going, and she picked up bits and pieces of what they were talking about. She felt better and better as she took bites of her Ceasar Salad and sips of her Pinot Grigio. She'd always been able to hold her booze, or at least to appear to be able to do so. She didn't appear drunk and got through a third glass before seeing how empty the pub had become.

She admitted to herself that she might be a wee bit woozy and ordered a coffee, which she drank black, and a slice of mousse cake, which she didn't finish. She paid the check, leaving a nice tip, and slowly left. In no time, she'd reached the Mercedes in the public parking lot around the corner. It had a ticket under a windshield wiper, and she cursed about that since she thought the two hours she'd paid for would be sufficient. It wasn't.

Thank goodness she didn't need to find her key fob buried in the recesses of her Coach shoulder bag. A touch on the door handle, a press of the ignition button, and she rolled out to the street. Unfortunately, she accelerated to beat a traffic light on Bloomingdale Road and the Benz fishtailed until it was abruptly stopped by that pole, her face bruised by the exploding airbag from the steering wheel.

Which is how her once beautiful red coupe ended up on a flatbed truck and how she ended up at the White Plains Police Station after being cleared by an EMT on site, where she was given her one phone call after she'd been fingerprinted and had her mug shots taken.

And that call went to Jane at her office. After telling her mother the fact of her arrest and that Eve was safe at home with the nanny, Jerri Astor, she gave a somewhat abbreviated story about how she came to be arrested, sliding over some of the details.

Jane immediately went to the office of a lawyer in the firm where she was a secretary. That lawyer arranged for a local attorney to show up at the police station to handle the legal side of things. Jane then decided to call Bridget. Everyone called Bridget, who was resigned to it. She worked only a few blocks away.

Jane knew she couldn't tell Amy or Peter yet. They'd immediately lose their minds about Eve. She'd let Bridget handle that part of the story. Which, of course, put

Bridget right in the middle of things. Other things, though, were moving too quickly for her to worry about that.

With scant information, Jane and Bridget Ubered to White Plains. Fran's newly-retained lawyer was just finishing up as they arrived and she was released about half-an-hour later. The three took another car to the house. Silently.

Once Fran was put to bed, Bridget called Amy. She gave as little information as she thought she could get away with. Fran had been in an accident. She wasn't hurt and Eve was at home when it happened. Fran is upset and at home. She is with us. Just don't panic.

Saying not to panic had the opposite effect, and Amy was on with Peter as soon as she hung up with Bridget. He got an Uber and picked Amy up and they headed up through the late afternoon traffic to Purchase.

When they arrived about an hour later, Fran was asleep. It was about seven, and Jerri was still there. The others spoke to the nanny about Fran and Eve.

Jerri assured them that she had never seen any sign that Fran was drinking excessively. She had a glass or two of wine during the week, as Jane knew, but never more than a couple at a time. She didn't keep hard liquor in the house. The nanny and Jane both assured the others that Fran hadn't and never would do anything to harm Eve.

"Then what the fuck was she doing getting drunk on a Tuesday afternoon and trying to drive home?" The others were taken aback by the vehemence of Bridget's words. Bridget was not. She lived with, and died with, babies who suffered through no fault of their own. Or their parents. Here was Fran, with advantages beyond imagination but who'd also seen the suffering of the same babies that she had, endangering her own.

"I would never hurt my baby."

The heads of all the others turned to see Fran standing in the center of the arched entrance to the room. She'd heard Bridget's outburst. "I WOULD NEVER HURT MY BABY." Repeated and louder, said as Jane rushed to her, the mother assuring the daughter that *I know, I know* when she got there. She led the sobbing Fran to the sofa, from which Amy and Bridget had quickly risen. They stood awkwardly off to the side, watching carefully, at times gauging how Peter and Jerri were reacting.

"I've never done anything like this before. I swear," Fran began when everyone else had settled, all but Jane still standing. Jane was sitting beside her daughter and holding her hand.

Fran had decided she needed to finally open up. It had all come together for her while she was sitting in that locked room at White Plains PD waiting for someone to save her and let her see her daughter again.

She took a deep breath, locking her eyes on a ceramic bowl that was on the coffee table. It was white with colorful paint strokes encircling it, and it held a collection of small gray stones.

"I went to the mall. After wandering around Nieman's, I went to the other stores. I didn't go into any, but all I could see were all these women, well-dressed Westchester women younger than me with their Gucci bags that weren't knock-offs and blown out hair chatting with one another as they passed me or came out of stores."

She leaned forward and removed a stone from the bowl. After rolling it between her fingers for a moment, she dropped it whence it had come.

"So, I'm thinking that I'd like to be doing that. I have a ton of money and I don't have a single friend I could chat about nothing with at the mall. I can't make fun of their awful taste and they can't envy me for my impeccable taste."

She gave a wan smile at this, the others not sure if she was joking.

"I have no friends." She looked at Bridget. "In the old days we were poor, Bridget and me and the other RNs, and we worked shit hours at what was too often a shit job."

Bridget nodded with her arms folded and said, "Can't go back, girl."

The others were carefully watching this interaction, and Fran nodded to the blonde woman she'd once felt so close to.

"No, Bridget. We can't go back."

She shot a glance at Peter and then returned it to the bowl of stones.

"I'm such a fucking cliché."

She stood. She walked towards Peter, and Amy stiffened. Fran turned her eyes to Amy. "Don't worry, Amy. I can't go back." She looked back at Peter. "But I so much wish I could go back and be a woman who wanted a good man and not a pot of money."

She walked past that *pot of money* and tapped his shoulder as she did and without another word left the room to go upstairs to her grand bedroom with its professionally curated décor and the walk-in closet in which there was not a single knock-off.

25.

IN THE AFTERMATH, JANE agreed to move into her daughter's house. Lord knows there was enough room! She had stayed for several nights after the arrest but after Fran begged and begged, she agreed to actually move in. It dramatically increased the time it took Jane to commute and a hired car came to pick her up and drive her to the train each morning and bring her home from the station each night, but she wanted to be close to whatever her daughter would become after the arrest.

It might have helped in some ways but couldn't alter the reality that Fran had no friends. She had all this money yet couldn't chat with *friends* on a quick late-night call or when going store-to-store. Because she had no friends.

The nurses she had spent time-off with in the old days were too busy and not interested in the *new Fran*. Some resented her for having violated a code among nurses. Nurses never looked down at other nurses for sleeping around; it went with the emotional turmoil of their daily lives. But to entrap a rich guy as everyone knew Fran did was beyond the pale. More than a few thought that Fran deserved to wallow alone in her big house in Purchase and few if any would exchange her life for Fran's. Money, house, red Mercedes coupe, and all. Even the heated pool and sauna.

Moreover, Jane was no longer the maternal comfort she'd once been. She paid her daughter rent—it was a matter of principle—and bought a used Honda but if the weather was alright she was leaving early and returning late on Sundays—parkway-to-bridge-to-Astoria—to see the many friends that *she* had in Queens.

Amy was nice enough now that she was allowed to hold Eve on her visits but she always had a tinge of anger or jealousy concerning whatever Fran's current and especially former relationship was with her husband. More than anything, Fran viewed Amy as tolerating her for Eve's sake. Not much of a foundation for igniting any sort of true friendship.

Bridget had somewhat gotten over what Fran did to Peter. But she was still so damn sanctimonious. Fucking St. Theresa of Lenox Hill. She couldn't avoid being like that, and Fran always resented it.

On the legal front, the lawyer in Jane's firm had chosen well. Fran's attorney was diligent about his client's options in handling the case. He arranged for a series of therapy sessions—which also helped by giving Fran a no-judgment space—and negotiated a deal with the district attorney regarding Fran's DUI arrest. She pled guilty to driving-while-ability-impaired when she accepted therapy and sobriety conditions for a year. She surrendered her driver's license for ninety days.

The sentence didn't require complete sobriety. Her therapist told the judge that Fran was capable of drinking in moderation and that to force her not to drink at all could have the effect of tempting her to drink too much. If she crossed a line with one drink, her thinking would be, why stop there?

The elephant remained in the room. Fran's isolation.

After talking it over with Peter and Amy following the arrest and plea-deal, Bridget offered Fran the job of Deputy Director of the Foundation. She also suggested that Fran sell the house in Purchase and buy a place in Queens. It would make the commute to her new job and for Jane to her old one far easier and would allow Jane to return to the comfortable neighborhood she lived in before joining her daughter in Westchester.

Within four months of the arrest, Fran bought a three-bedroom condo in a newly-built eight-story apartment building in Astoria. From its terrace, one could see the New York skyline and it was only three blocks from the N train. The subway was faster than using a car service and they both enjoyed the anonymous rush-hour camaraderie. Depending, of course, on how crowded the car was but since in the morning they got on at one of the first stops, they usually got seats.

So, when they were back in the city—as Queens technically but not emotionally is—Eve's mom and grandma left her each morning in the care of Jerri—the nanny who had the third room in the Astoria apartment—and took the subway into the city.

It turned out that as was the case with Bridget, Fran proved conscientious and adept at her job. She became the point-of-contact between the Foundation and grant recipients. She enjoyed traveling to the labs of institutions in the tri-state area that were developing possible treatments and preventatives. Whatever lingering thoughts of Peter that had once fueled her self-satisfaction had faded to nothing. She was reinvigorated by the move to Queens and the job in midtown Manhattan. And she'd become a master of distinguishing between men in search of a serious, honest relationship—which was in some respects ironic given her own history—and those who only wanted to get into her bed or get into her bank account or, more often, both. Even though she had a one-year-old.

Things improved further and on an unexpected front when Fran attended a demonstration at a company in eastern Nassau County, New York. She'd reviewed the grant proposal with Bridget. Both thought it promising, but it would take a bit of time and investigation to know whether there was any there there.

As usual, Fran went to the company's dog-and-pony show for the demonstration. She'd attended enough of these to zone out the bullshit that usually permeated them, most often by a sales or money guy. (Or the occasional sales or money *gal.*) She knew enough to withhold judgment until one of the people who actually knew the product, flaws and all, got up to speak. They were usually a bit nerdy, quite intense, and shy but passionate. The ones who worked eighty-hour weeks surviving on ridiculous amounts of ramen noodles, caffeine and Red Bull. Often to the horror of the sales or money person, they too casually mentioned actual, significant issues in the development.

On this day, that person was Barry Peters. A Dartmouth B.S. with a biochemistry Ph.D. from Columbia. He'd probably given the pitch three or four times to venture capitalists and foundations. Always seeking money. Always turned down.

Fran found his nervousness endearing and his knowledge absolute. She stopped listening and taking notes after five or six minutes. She didn't need to hear more. She knew enough to know she would recommend to Bridget and the Foundation board that they do a deep dive in the expectation of giving it money and with it getting a share of the company. The Foundation obtained equity in companies as a source of future funding. It was a trick Bridget had learned from Peter and his incubator experience.

Fran was careful not to be overly enthusiastic about the presentation since there was still a bit more examination that would be required and because it was not her decision, however much the review committee had come to rely on her opinion. At the end, she assured Barry Peters that the Foundation would be considering his company moving forward.

And she made sure to get his number.

26.

WHILE FRAN'S LIFE WAS bouncing between its lows and its increasingly frequent highs, Amy grew and grew and...

Her pregnancy had become common knowledge even to the boutiques and overpriced eateries in East Hampton. And to the liquor store in Sag Harbor to which the house sent its orders, which did not ask for quite so many bottles of wine as it used to.

At seven months along, she took an early maternity leave from Enswich & Taylor, leaving open the question of when, and if, she would return. She loved the work and had been promoted but decided to focus on her baby, which she knew would be a boy, leaving whether she'd ever return up in the air.

A grand and expensively catered baby shower was held at the Apartment, jointly curated by Bridget and Fran. *What do you get for the mother who has everything?* was a not uncommon question among guests, but all managed to touch Amy Edgar with their generosity with the caveat that she had secretly called each of the guests and asked that they not overspend and that their gifts would be sent to a single mothers' organization in the Bronx for distribution for mothers and children who would be more in need than her baby would ever be. Those restrictions were not, however, reflected in the pictures posted on Instagram and other social media. They showed the world that a good time was had by all.

And then the waiting and anticipation were over.

On April 3, Peter Edgar, Jr. was born at Lenox Hill Hospital.

He clocked in at a solid 7 lbs. and 14 ozs. Mother and baby were doing well. And their picture appeared on Page Six in *The Post* and on the Instagram feeds of several Upper East Side influencers.

27

FRAN WAS GETTING serious about Barry Peters, and he about her. But she was more fragile than either of them realized. She'd had several serious relationships before meeting Peter, but they inevitably faltered on her long hours and peculiar schedule and on her sometimes...difficult personality.

Then there was the disaster of missed and regretted opportunities with Peter, a disaster she very slowly understood was entirely her fault. After that, she was not fit for male companionship for an extended period, though she did have a few quickies, most particularly with the doctor in Westchester.

Things loosened, though, after she'd gotten Barry Peters's number.

She didn't call until after the Foundation had accepted the grant application from his company and each *i* was dotted and each *t* was crossed. Fran gave it a few days and then called him and they agreed to meet the following Saturday.

Things went well on that date and even better on the ones that followed. On the fourth, they met for dinner not too far from his apartment, and they both knew that proximity was a proxy for what they wanted to do after dessert. And they spent the rest of the night at his place and in his bed after Fran gave her mother a not-too-subtle message that she wasn't coming home that night and that Jane or Jerri would have to take care of Eve.

It had been too long for Fran after the booty calls she'd had with that oncologist before the whole DUI incident. And it was good for Fran and Barry the next Saturday, when they didn't even bother to go out for dinner but ordered take out Chinese, enjoying a post-coital feast sitting on the floor in the kitchen, he in jeans and nothing else and she in one of his oversized Columbia T-shirts and nothing else.

Fran, though, did something stupid and destructive. She had cheated on Peter and she began to wonder whether Barry would cheat on her. There was absolutely no evidence of this. In the following few days, though, it gained weight in her mind and by the time they were out at a restaurant in Astoria on Thursday night and he had gone to the men's room before dessert, his phone pinged.

She had no excuse.

She looked around the restaurant to see if anyone was looking in her direction. Seeing no one, she pulled Barry's phone along the tablecloth so she could reach it. It was unlocked and she hit the message icon. She clicked on the first message and began to scroll through the history with the *Melissa* who had sent it.

She wondered whether he'd ever mentioned this Melissa from his lab and couldn't recall. *Was she the pretty young thing who'd helped him at the dog-and-pony show where they met and where Fran had been so impressed? Did she look at him with a little more attention and admiration than was appropriate at a business event?*

The messages were all work related but in her mind they seemed a bit too flirty. He'd never given any indication that he had something to hide on his phone. When they were together, he'd never quickly changed to a different app when a text appeared. At his place, he'd never jumped up with his phone cradled in his hand to go to the bathroom or get something from the kitchen.

She turned the phone around and pushed it back across the cloth. He was just coming back and the waiter had just put the dessert and decaf coffees on the table. He restored his napkin and told her how good the chocolate mousse looked.

As he poured milk into his coffee, she didn't move.

"What's wrong, honey?" he asked as he put the creamer on the table. He reached for a packet of sugar but stopped before he opened it.

"Seriously, Fran. What the hell is wrong?"

"Ask Melissa," she said. She pushed her chair back hard. It almost toppled. She threw her napkin on the table and turned and wound her way past the other tables to the door and was gone.

He sat stunned. By then, he'd learned enough of her background to understand her nervousness and insecurities. But this? *Melissa?* What did his gay lab assistant have to do with anything?

He rushed after her, handing his credit card to the maître d' as he swept by him, promising to return for it, and was out onto the sidewalk.

He caught a glimpse of her nearly a block ahead. She was going to her apartment. He broke into an awkward sprint up Steinway Street and caught up to her when she was about half-a-block from her building.

At first, she ripped her arm from his grasp but then turned.

She was crying, and he reached his arms around her. She leaned her head against his shoulder and he ran his hands up and down her back.

There was a 24-hour diner on the corner. They found a booth and sat across from each other in the red vinyl benches. Each asked for coffee though neither intended to drink it. Instead, they moved the mugs around across the Formica top like props that could keep their hands busy.

It was awkward but they finally began to talk.

She confessed to her breach of his privacy but said she couldn't resist and then her mind was in such a state that

117

she thought the worst of every one of the texts with this Melissa.

He explained who Melissa was and especially that she was married to a woman she'd met at Hofstra. "I was at their wedding," he said, his tone lightening when he saw how his description of his co-worker seemed to clear away something in Fran's mind. He convinced her that it was nothing but the playful text banter of nerds in a stressful environment. Turning deadly serious, he added that if she'd have him, he'd commit himself to her completely.

Mollified, Fran signaled their waitress and ordered a slice of lemon meringue pie. It was delivered in the middle of the table with two forks. He slid his hand towards her and she slid hers towards him. The tears stopped and his finger dabbed the final one that was drifting down her cheek. She grabbed the hand and kissed that finger and then turned to the sugary pie and it was among the best desserts either of them could ever remember having.

She let him rush back to the original restaurant to settle the tab and collect his Visa card. While he was doing that, she called Jane and told her she might be a little late—a phrase Jane had long since come to *understand*—and she let him drive out to his place in Port Washington where they had some pretty excellent make-up sex.

But things were not the same after that for either of them. She was alternatively begging for forgiveness and accusing him of an imaginary transgression. *Maybe,* she thought, *this co-worker was bi- and not gay and scratching her straight itch with Barry*. There was no evidence of this and she didn't even give him the chance to deny this insane accusation, but that barely slowed her down in those moments when she'd thrown herself into jealousy and despair.

A month later, after one final time when she hung up on him mid-sentence, he texted her to suggest that maybe it made more sense for them to stop seeing one another. This sent Fran back into a place she didn't want to see, let alone enter again. She called Bridget and on the Monday after the text and after she'd blocked his number, the two sat down in the Foundation's conference room to talk.

Bridget had difficulty wrapping her head around Fran. They'd known each other for years and were friends in what had become a turbulent dance at Lenox Hill. Then she'd done what she'd done with Peter and it took a long time, a very long time, for Bridget to have anything to do with her. And when she did, it was entirely because Fran was the mother of Peter's daughter.

Things had been rocky since then but they somehow had put this history aside enough so that they could work together at the Foundation, where Bridget was Fran's boss.

Fran remained complicated and conflicted about everything. In the end, though, she found a refuge in Eve. As if her entire life was seeking someone who would love her unconditionally and that person was the daughter she carried and gave birth to. But it didn't fill in the loneliness and the need for a different type of love. A physical love and a physical connection with someone.

So, when they sat down, and not liking having to say it, Bridget told Fran that she had to get her head out of her ass and get back to work. Fran was good at her job. The episode with Barry, or more accurately episodes, had put her on her heels and started her spiraling. Now she was gun-shy about everything. Miserable and self-pitying. Especially when something with his lab's logo crossed her desk. Plus, she was in one of her feeling-sorry-for-myself modes.

In the days immediately after Barry's break-up text, though, Fran was more open than usual and after Bridget told her to cut-the-crap, she also stood and told Fran they were going for a walk.

Clicking in her Louboutin heels in contrast to Bridget's more sensible flats, they walked to Rockefeller Center's promenade. Topiary elephants had been set up along the stretch that sloped down from Fifth Avenue, and the two found spots to sit among the brightly colored tourists speaking a mélange of languages.

Side-by-side, arms touching, they turned to face each other and bent their heads close to maintain secrecy in their conversation.

"Why do I always fuck it up?" Fran asked, as honest a thing as she'd ever said. Bridget, St. Bridget, reached for her subordinate's hand.

"You fuck it up because you don't trust yourself. You and Peter could have been good together, but you jumped at the chance to grab some of his money."

"I got Eve out of the deal."

"The best thing to ever happen to you. I know that." Bridget paused for effect. "You trust yourself to be her mom, right?"

"It's not about trusting myself. It just *is*."

"Exactly. You didn't trust Barry to love—"

"That's what I mean. Always fucking things up."

"No. You didn't trust him to love you so when you got nervous you blew the thing up."

"It's not like there wasn't evidence."

"Which turned out to be no evidence at all. He explained it and you accepted what he said and then you just couldn't let it go." Bridget felt how exasperating this all was and her voice quickened. "You couldn't trust a man you thought you loved. This is all on you, Fran."

"I think I do love him," Fran said. "That's what I mean. I always fuck it up. And I'm so lonely."

"Things are better now that you're back in Queens, right?" Bridget asked.

"Yeah, but I always wanted to get out of there."

"Why?"

"It's just what people are supposed to do." She turned away from her boss, staring ahead.

Bridget soldiered on. "Because you think if you leave, you'll be better than those you leave behind."

"And didn't you leave the Bronx by staying at Peter's place on Park Avenue?" Fran challenged Bridget.

"Fran. Don't go there. You know I've never run from my roots."

Bridget was suddenly very pissed, and Fran knew she had crossed a line.

"I know. I'm sorry. I didn't mean that the way it came out. But the guys in Astoria. They're just a bunch of schmucks. Talking about the Mets and the Giants and the Knicks..."

"Look. All I can tell you is to keep your mind open. If you like someone, you like someone. More importantly, if you *love* someone, you love someone. Don't overthink."

Bridget knew how hypocritical she was being. She never actually had had a boyfriend. She had gone out on dates, but none grew into a relationship. Now she was giving relationship advice to a woman who had infinitely more experience than she did. A bolt grazed her: she'd never actually...loved someone. And, worse, no one had loved her.

She put this uncomfortable revelation aside. She had been pulled in as a mentor or friend or confidante by Fran and she was confident that she could help her.

They say insanity is doing the same thing again and again and expecting a different result, she thought. In love, maybe Fran was insane. Not in a good way.

For her part, Fran seemed almost resigned to repeating the same mistake. Bridget, though, was right. Fran had made a mess of Barry Peters. If she could just stop overthinking. Or maybe it was just a fear of having happiness inevitably turn to grief. Maybe she just needed to pull her head out of her ass.

Bridget tapped Fran's hand. "I hope I helped," she said. The two rose and began the walk back to the office. Fran promised Bridget she would try to conquer her doubts and insecurities. Neither knew if she would. And they returned to their offices and Fran seemed to get back on an even keel at work. She continued going to dog-and-pony shows of grant applicants and continued to provide good advice to Bridget concerning what she saw and heard.

By the beginning of summer, the two were working as well together as ever. Shortly after she spoke with Bridget, Fran called Barry. She asked to meet him for drinks, and he suggested a small place near his office on the Island. Along the water in Port Washington. It went well, and they agreed to a fresh slate. Fran again recalled that she could fall in love with this man and why she might want to.

Part 2

1.

BY EARLY JULY, with Fran having recovered her bearings at the Foundation and gotten back on track at least at the office, Bridget finally took a one-week semi-vacation at the Hamptons house. It wouldn't be a *true* vacation because everyone knew she couldn't keep her hands out completely, but she promised them all that at most, at the very, very most, she'd only review things for a couple of hours before noon and that then she'd actually put that all aside and bask in the luxury of Peter and Amy's largesse.

She drove out late on Friday afternoon with Amy and Petey safely ensconced in his baby seat in the backseat of the Porsche. Peter followed a few hours later in the Aston, with the top down and his music blasting far louder than Amy would ever have allowed and much to the chagrin of those he was passing or who were passing him. He'd leave the convertible for Bridget and return on Sunday night with his family in the Cayenne.

Matters passed smoothly for the rest of the day, but Sunday morning found everyone's phones pinging with increasingly ominous alerts from the National Weather Service with all sorts of ominous warnings about angry weather crossing along the length of Long Island. *Batten down the hatches!*

Peter and Amy decided to make a run for home with Petey, heading out before noon on Sunday. They questioned this decision several times when they were crawling along the Long Island Expressway not long after they merged into it at Exit 70.

This was why Peter had a Porsche SUV but as they drove slowly along the Interstate with the wipers flapping at an insane rate, their greatest fear was the Hamptons idiots who thought—nay, *knew*—they were immune to the laws of physics in their G-wagons or Lambos or Range Rovers that would enjoy concierge treatment in the garages where they were *boarded* should they successfully make it back to their Manhattan stables.

In the end, though, the trio of Edgars made it across the Triborough with Peter at the wheel and Amy and Petey in the back seat listening to the sixties rock that Peter found relaxing as he drove, although not nearly so loud as when he drove alone. By the time they'd stopped in front of their building, two doormen were ready for them with large black umbrellas to escort them under the awning into the lobby and one of them drove the Porsche, its mustard yellow looking not so appealing in the raging storm, to the nearby parking garage.

Shortly after they were safely home, with the fury of the storm dumping clusters of rain on East Hampton, Amy called Bridget to let her know they'd reached the apartment damp but in one piece.

Amy texted.

> {Amy:} *We all love you. Please please please forget everything, and I mean everything, and enjoy your vacation. You deserve it.*

> {Amy:} *Please!!!!* ☺ ☺ 🩶

Bridget responded with her own 🩶

By morning at the eastern end of the south fork of Long Island, the rain and thunder had drifted east over the open Atlantic and Bridget awoke to the peace of a new, sunny day with a whole large house and its deck and pool all to herself.

She walked downstairs barefoot in her pajama bottoms dappled with yellow daisies against a blue background and an oversized dark blue T-shirt that said *Nurses Have Seen It All* and her blonde hair a dangling tangled mess. She went straight to the kitchen counter. She pushed the button to start brewing the coffee she'd set up before she'd climbed into her plush bed the night before. While the machine started gurgling, she walked over to the window.

The Atlantic had calmed from the get-thee-to-an-Ark fury it had been when she'd last seen it as the Sunday dusk had settled into night. Instead, it had the innocence of someone awakening and realizing that what had flashed through her brain as she slept was only a nightmare, if a terrifying one at that.

When she heard the coffee machine bing, she stepped to it and filled her maroon Lenox Hill Hospital mug with the steaming brew and collected it. She returned to the sliding doors and slipped on her pair of sandals that was among a line of everyone else's and stepped onto the still damp deck.

It'd be hot but not quite yet, and the humidity that had plagued the Edgars during their stay was gone. She looked out and down at the beach, empty except for a runner who was moving away to the west, shirtless and barefoot along the beach's edge, his feet being cleansed by the final strains of the incoming waves.

For her, though, the sand was too damp for a stroll and she needed to check some early Monday morning emails. But not before she poured the remains of the coffee into a carafe and made a couple of slices of wheat toast, which she slathered with butter—a bad habit she grew up with thanks to her Irish dad but refused to part with—and carried the mug in one hand and the plated toast in the other and went to the study where she could get the things she told herself she had to take care of out of the way.

After a check of her work emails, none of which was urgent and most of which had also gone to Fran, she called her second-in-command to check in and was told in no uncertain terms that everything was fine in the office and that it would be greatly appreciated if she would stop bothering people who had real work to do.

Thus chastened, Bridget had enjoyed the luxury of falling down various of the internet's rabbit holes, piling up page after page of cute Shih Tzus and explanations for why this supplement will kill you and why that will allow for an eternal erection and stories of how couples in their sixties had met cute thirty years before.

So, there she was, in a room with a top-of-the-line computer in one of the finest houses in all of America watching bodega cats asleep on bags of kitty litter. And she loved it.

But she had drained the last vestiges of her coffee and after three or four attempts, managed to get off her ass and down to the kitchen for a refill.

The day was in its full glory. She carried her replenished mug to the door to the deck, put her sandals back on, and stepped out. There was more activity on the beach than there had been, but things were still way too damp for anything of significance.

It was strange, then, to see a lone woman sitting on that sand. She wasn't even on a towel or a blanket. She was in a pair of khaki shorts that must be soaked but she wasn't moving, just staring out to the ocean. Her arms embraced her legs as she sat motionless and hatless.

She was too far away for Bridget to be able to make out anything else about her. It was clear that wherever she was, she wanted to be there alone. Bridget would let this strange interloper be.

The deck's furniture was damp. The cushions for the furniture were in a large container off to the side, protected from the weather, but Bridget would wait until later to pull them out and place them on the chairs and beach lounges. She went back inside to take a shower.

She lingered for longer than she may ever had beneath the rainfall nozzle. It was liberating to be on vacation for once. She turned her head up and let the droplets paint her face and then ran her hands over herself, immersed in the touches of her fingers as they wandered and dawdled. She concentrated on herself for a change and found herself pushed over the edge of pleasure, which forced her to turn off the spray so she could recover and not fall into a perpetually smiling and satisfied heap that the cleaning staff would discover when they came by early the next morning.

Instead, she said aloud, slightly out of breath, *I did not see that coming* as she stepped from the shower and lifted a towel to dry herself. It was a plush towel and she lingered again with it before turning to the desteamed mirror and staring at the not-unattractive woman looking back as she brushed her hair out and wrapped it into a practical ponytail while she contemplated how she would spend this first day in paradise alone.

It must have been fully thirty minutes later when she returned to the ground floor in her own pair of khaki shorts and a light blue Lauren polo shirt. She carried her personal laptop under one arm and held her treasured Lenox Hill mug in her other hand.

She walked straight to the door to the deck and, after again putting her sandals on, stepped out. It was warmer now. The day would clearly be a hot one.

Before going to get the cushions for at least one of the chairs, she saw that the strange woman was still sitting. She didn't seem to have moved. There were more people streaming onto the beach, some with families, but she remained precisely where she'd been. Staring out to the Atlantic's nothingness.

That woman was Evelyn Manners. She wore a cream-colored blouse tinged with lace. Her blonde hair was in an ill-constructed bun. Her ass was wet. Not damp. Wet from her sitting for so long. She didn't care. It was the first day of her own weeklong vacation, a vacation she was taking alone because...there was no one else. She was one of four women from her job—at Chase Bank— who'd gotten a July time share for a place in East Hampton well away from the beach. A not-quite-affordable-but-worth-it part of the town.

Her car, a six-year-old maroon BMW 5 Series that she bought two years earlier when it came off of someone else's lease, was parked on a street not that far away that dead-ended at the beach.

She listened to and watched the waves coming and going.

In the dampness, the waves that lapped against the sand again and again and then withdrew had a hypnotic effect on Evelyn, leading her to think about herself deeply in a way she rarely did. It seemed appropriate. The kisses and the withdrawals. The energy spent each time the salty water hit the beach.

Out of nowhere she recalled long forgotten lines from Shelley that had somehow become fixed in her mind in some undergraduate English Lit course she'd taken as a sophomore or junior.

And the sunlight clasps the earth
  And the moonbeams kiss the sea:
What is all this sweet work worth
  If thou kiss not me?

Ironic. She'd never had someone whose kiss she was desperate for, truly desperate as a woman should be at least once in her life and doubted that she ever would.

Evelyn Manners was very pretty. Her one unnatural feature was the expensive blonde hair in that messy bun, her light-brown roots slightly peeking through. She bought her hair but everything else was given to her by God.

She'd grown up in Chappaqua, an affluent suburb in upper Westchester County. With her MBA, she toiled in a nondescript department at Chase Bank's headquarters on Park Avenue in midtown Manhattan. She was 5' 8" and had a toned body. Nice boobs, which were natural. A very nice face with a slightly hooked nose, which divided large sapphire eyes and sat above a pair of large lips.

As she sat, she long contemplated that little had happened to her since her engagement had blown up after she'd refused the request—it turned out it was more of a *demand*—her fiancé had made in their bed following what had been a happy Valentine's Day dinner. By that week's end, she was single again. She blamed herself. So did he and his friends and just about everyone else.

That was over a year before she was sitting on the expensive East Hampton sand. She hadn't had a steady boyfriend since. She was finally tired of going to her apartment alone and more tired of going to someone else's apartment for a one-night hookup.

Kissing and withdrawing. Much like the ocean's waves.

She was smart but her looks were her curse. She was content to be an okay student in high school. Which meant she ended up at an okay college where she did okay and got her MBA from an okay business school. Which explains why she worked in a nondescript department deep in the bowels of Chase. She spent too much on her apartment on the Upper East Side and was paying too much for the quarter-share in the Hamptons and for that BMW she drove rarely and had to garage.

Her house share was for the month, but the others were back in the city, and this was the first weekday of her week-long vacation. She didn't like being alone and she started to anticipate Friday night, when her mates would be back in the Hamptons and they could all go to some party to get drunk and laid.

Looking at the lonely days ahead and depressed, she didn't care that her ass cheeks were very uncomfortably soaked. She was increasingly hypnotized by the waves rolling over the sand. Each pushed her deeper and deeper into herself. Paralyzed. Crying without realizing it. Even wondering, though just for a flickering moment, what it would be like to just walk herself into oblivion in an ocean drowning.

But she quickly discarded the notion. It would be too much a cliché in her depressing life.

She was startled back to the here-and-now and for a moment frightened when a stranger sat next to her and put her hand on her shoulder.

"You want to tell me about it?"

Evelyn shook from the unexpected interruption and looked to her side, glad it was a woman's voice she heard but still uncomfortable.

She put her hand above her eyes so she could see who this asshole was. It turned out to be Bridget Casey. After seeing that the unnamed girl hadn't moved, Bridget had gone down the thirty steps that led from the house's deck to the beach.

She had sat down. Uninvited.

Evelyn turned, startled at the interruption. Bridget reached her hand to the other's arm and smiled as she repeated her question.

"Seriously, do you want to talk about it? It's not every day that I see someone sitting in wet sand and not moving for like half-an-hour."

Suppressing a *who-the-fuck-are-you?*, Evelyn instead asked, "How long do you have?" She was trying to be light in how she said it but it had a core of pain.

They rose, each swiping their bottoms to brush off some sand, and then stepped towards the water before skirting the waves as they turned right and walked west, keeping some distance between themselves, and the sun behind them.

Evelyn knew plenty of people, but none were true friends. This woman was a stranger. They exchanged names. Just firsts. Evelyn realized that whatever she said to this passing figure would allow her to relieve herself of at least some of her demons without risking repercussion or judgment from someone who in the least bit mattered to her. Like a priest.

So, as they continued, Bridget kept her promise and listened. The pair carried their sandals as they walked, letting them swing back and forth in time with their steps, and looked down at the sand and up to the far horizon where the beach and the ocean disappeared in the distance.

A few times, they each turned back, seeing in their footprints the slightly varying traces of where they'd been. Sometimes looking at the Atlantic. Nodding to those passing and heading whence they'd come.

Evelyn spoke like the waves, sentence upon sentence of frustration and inadequacy and unhappiness, coming without respite, one after the other.

Eventually, they turned to head back towards where Evelyn had spent all of that time on her butt. When they neared the starting point, it was almost noon. Bridget asked her new friend if she had time for a bite of lunch. Evelyn saw no reason to say *no* and realized she was quite famished.

"Yes," she said, and was shocked when Bridget turned to the left and led her up a staircase that went directly from the beach. As she followed Bridget up the steps, the house itself seemed to rise from the dunes. It was huge. Bridget said she might be able to get something dry for a stunned Evelyn to put on, and the two went into the great room together as if it was the most natural thing in the world.

Who is this woman? Evelyn asked herself. She must be famous to afford this.

"Help yourself to some water," Bridget said nonchalantly as they passed the kitchen. "I'll be right down."

Just like that, she was going up the stairs and before Evelyn had the chance to fill the glass she'd taken down from the cabinet she finally found with it, Bridget was back. She held a towel in one hand and a pair of shorts and a blue Manhattanville T-shirt in the other.

"You can use the bathroom down here to dry yourself off," she said as she handed the items to Evelyn. "I'm sorry, but I don't have any…new panties for you so you'll just have to commando it until I can get your stuff washed and dried. It'll take no time and we can enjoy some lunch in the meantime."

The two were comfortable on the deck half an hour later. They'd made sandwiches from the bread and cold cuts that Amy had picked up at the market in town for Bridget's stay. Bridget made a fresh pot of coffee, and the two had placed cushions on the deck furniture. Evelyn had opened the umbrella that poked through the middle of the round table and put placemats out.

Finally, Evelyn asked what she'd been dying to.

"This is your place?"

Bridget shook her head. "My dad's a cop and my mom's a nurse. This is not my place. It's a friend's. It's where I'm working and being lazy this week."

Evelyn's first thought was just who it was that was this blonde's friend who had a mansion overlooking the Atlantic with a staircase that went directly to the beach.

Bridget smiled. She hastened to explain that it was Peter and Amy Edgar's and that she was their friend and also worked for their foundation in Rockefeller Center.

Evelyn accepted this.

To bring her guest down to earth, Bridget asked where she'd parked. It wasn't far, and the two walked to bring the BMW over to the house's pebbled circular driveway.

They were quiet when they returned to the deck. The sun was strong in the now cloudless sky. They moved off to the side, to a pair of beach lounges close to one another. Bridget went inside to the bathroom on the ground floor and grabbed a large plastic bottle of sunblock. When she returned, she handed it to Eveyln, who slathered it on her face and neck, and when she got it back, Bridget did the same to herself.

The two then reclined so they were half sitting/half lying in the sun. Bridget put another umbrella up for shade. Only a few people were heard from the beach against the steady rhythm of the waves pounding the shore.

Before long, and although it was barely two, Bridget decided not to wait and went in, returning with a bottle of primo Chardonnay and two glasses with their stems between her fingers and bulbs facing down. She'd uncorked the bottle inside and nearly filled the glasses without objection from Evelyn.

"We're both on vacation," she said as she sat, holding her glass out so her guest could clink it.

Once settled, they at first were quiet, each savoring the chilled wine in little sips. Then Bridget spoke about herself. While it wasn't much, Evelyn was fascinated.

A few times, Evelyn expressed real surprise and her *no way*s received a gentle *way* in response. Finally, Evelyn just put her glass on the small table that was between them and laid back on her beach lounge and simply listened to Bridget's slight Bronx accent and her improbable tale of how the hell she ended up staying at this house for her vacation.

It was strange. The combination of what Bridget was saying and how sweetly, unpretentiously she was saying it. How her words flowed and the way her hands moved while she spoke with a subtle passion. Her natural empathy was enhanced by her work as a nurse, a job Evelyn could not imagine herself undertaking.

Evelyn closed her eyes. Eventually, Bridget did the same, leaning back and going silent as they heard the waves and the sound of distant families romping in the surf and on the beach.

The spontaneous guest let the sound of the ocean come to her. Always another wave, always another chance to not fuck up. Then Bridget heard Evelyn snoring lightly. She turned to look at her guest. *So pretty. So unfair.* According to what Evelyn admitted, she'd let it control her. Consume her. School-to-school, job-to-job. Coasting. No wonder she was lost on the beach. Longing to be washed to a new life wherever the Atlantic might take her.

Bridget went into the kitchen. It was nearing six. She gave Amy a call and told her about Evelyn, asking if it was okay if she stayed for the week. Without any hesitation, Amy said that was fine with her and Peter.

Music played in the background. WFUV through Alexa. Bridget lightly hummed and even joined in on songs she liked. She grabbed a head of lettuce and ripped it apart before putting it in the spinner. Her plan was to throw some onions and tomatoes into butter and olive oil for an easy-peasy sauce. She chopped the onions and the tomatoes, and some garlic, and tossed them into a pan as she put water into a pot and dumped some salt in.

With the sauce, a bit of parsley and basil tossed in, simmering and the water not yet boiled, she took her glass out to the deck. Evelyn reacted by waking. She had been out for a while. "Hey sleepyhead," her host said.

Evelyn moved slowly and then smiled and yawned and stretched, trying to reorient herself to where she was. She reached for the glass Bridget had re-filled and took a sip. She could get used to this. Both women sat on the deck, ignoring and obsessed with one another in equal parts. Till the timer went off and Bridget rushed in, leaving *I hope you like spaghetti* in her wake.

Evelyn joined her in the kitchen, tossing the salad and putting oil and vinegar on it while Bridget drained the pasta and returned it to the pot then poured the sauce and a bit of the water from the pot over it, adding lots of butter and grated Romano cheese. That done, she put the contents in a large bowl with a pair of wooden utensils and brought it to the large table on the deck, where Evelyn had laid two place-settings. Evelyn brought the wine and the salad, and they sat next to one another beneath the umbrella to enjoy the view and the air.

After Bridget said Amy okayed it, Evelyn slept at the house that night. Sometime between two and two-thirty, Evelyn was awakened by the waves. She was used to nighttime Manhattan traffic. She wasn't used to nighttime rhythmic waves. The moon was full, and the house was lit up enough so that she could make her way to the deck without turning on a light, the crashing waves drawing her. She stepped out.

She heard a slight snoring. Bridget. She too in a long maroon T-Shirt. It was warm but not too hot to sleep in the open air. Bridget's face was to the side, her chest slowly rising and falling. There was enough light for Evelyn to see this woman, and she quietly sat and looked. Maybe stared. She wasn't sure what she felt about her, but it was *something*. She let her sleep as she sat, looking out at the Atlantic and the moon's reflection. It had been an amazing day and she too drifted off.

Some hours later, Bridget felt the burning from the rising sun on her head and tried to wave it away. She was quickly awake and heard Evelyn to her right, again lightly snoring. It was Bridget's turn to stare at a beautiful woman. There was something about her. Damaged, yes. She might come to like her if she allowed herself to be herself and like herself. She woke her with a kiss to the forehead and, again, *sleepyhead*.

It embarrassed Evelyn, again. She shook and followed her friend inside, and after Bridget peed Evelyn did too and when she got back to the kitchen, Bridget had the coffee on. Peter had a high-end Italian machine with dials and buttons and lights, but Amy was the only one who knew how to use it, so Bridget resorted to the simple Braun drip machine.

It wasn't yet seven. No clouds. It would be warm, probably hot, but not humid. They were both a bit woozy but decided not to go back to their beds. They headed to the deck, with their coffees and their Special Ks.

Quiet. Evelyn put the umbrella up.

"You don't have to," Bridget began, "but I could use a break. What do you say about hanging with me this morning?"

Evelyn, of course, said *yes*. She had no plans, and she liked this woman. They hopped into the Aston and Bridget put the roof down. She reached to the floor of the back seat and pulled out a pair of straw hats with wide brims and chinstraps and she gave one to Evelyn and off they went.

They were soon in nearby and more subtly pretentious Bridgehampton before swinging north. They found a parking spot in front of the American Hotel on Sag Harbor's Main Street and surveyed the area, stopping in for some fun at the boutiques with dresses and accessories that neither of them could afford but that cost nothing to try on.

They got sandwiches and iced tea at a deli on a side street and found a seat in the small group of tables out front. Bridget suggested that Evelyn stay at the house for the rest of the week.

Evelyn said, "But I thought you wanted to be alone."

Bridget coyly said, "Yeah, but that was before I met you and realized it'd be lots more fun being together."

And so it was. Bridget made a quick call to Amy and got her approval. She and Evelyn headed south to Evelyn's rental, where she grabbed some clothes. Her roommates weren't due out until late Friday, and she texted the organizing one to let her know what was going on.

Evelyn was embarrassed when Bridget saw an expensive but often-worn summer cocktail dress among her things. It was what she would wear if she found

137

someone who would want to be seen with her at a party. She had never been to a party at a house on the scale of Peter Edgar's but some came close and she wasn't above being a piece of eye candy and above having sex in the back seat of a Range Rover at one of the sex-in-the-backseat-of-a-high-end-SUV dead-ends clustered near the ocean that by morning would be cluttered with used condoms, the occupants of each one politely ignoring the presence of the others.

All Bridget did when she noticed the dress, though, was smile; she knew its purpose. She said Evelyn should include it in the stuff for Peter's. Just in case. Evelyn, though, just left it behind.

The two stopped for lunch in town and went back to the house. Ignoring her promise to minimize working, Bridget could not help herself and refused to put aside work she thought needed to be done. She told her guest to make herself at home as she went into the den.

What to do? Evelyn hadn't planned out the week. Her vague plans were mostly to drive around and go to a bar a couple of nights.

Things were so very different now from what they were when she had developed those plans. She pulled out her tablet, went to Bridget's office to get the WiFi password, and thought about a book she never got around to reading. Austen's *Persuasion*. She'd seen a TV version and with good intentions had brought it with her as one of her *beach reads*. It was quite the contrast to the one with the colorful cover and the cartoonish woman in a hat and pretty dress and some kind of splashy drink in her hand. That one now didn't seem quite up to Bridget's deck, so Austen it would be. If only to see what all the fuss was about.

On a beach lounge and beneath the umbrella on the deck with an iced tea concoction Bridget had made for her, she struggled through some of the book family's biographical junk before beginning her connection with the book's star and was well into it when Bridget called to her from the kitchen to get off her ass and help with dinner.

She closed the book using a finger as a bookmark until she could get a piece of paper to take over and went in to earn her keep.

2.

UNTIL FRIDAY, BRIDGET worked more than she'd promised herself that she would and couldn't spend much time with Evelyn during the day. Evelyn regretted this but it seemed to make Bridget happy so she didn't complain. Each morning, she went for a short run after the two had a light breakfast of cereal and coffee together. She ended her runs in town, where she picked up a copy of *The Times* and a few bagels or Danish to share with Bridget. While they had the paper on their various devices, she liked the feel and sight of *The Times* sections strewn about a room.

Instead of a need or desire to drive from town-to-town, during the day, Evelyn was content to sit in the great room or on the deck with her novel, about a woman who feared she would die alone after being persuaded to reject the man she loved because he was *without prospects*. Half an ear was spent listening for the den door to open, and when it did, she turned to see if Bridget was coming to the kitchen and she would smile if she was.

This was the pattern. They would have lunch together—Evelyn either made sandwiches or picked up something in town when she got the paper—and chatted for twenty or thirty minutes on the deck with iced teas. Bridget returned to her office and Evelyn returned to her novel. What a fool her heroine, Anne, had been but Evelyn understood her, Anne's, fear for making the leap. And Anne was paying the price, fearing the one she loved's indifference to her and that he, Captain Wentworth, had moved on.

Evelyn herself had moved on from her broken engagement. That marriage would have been a disaster to her, she realized, especially after that Valentine's Day night when her fiancé revealed a part of his character that he'd managed to keep hidden. Marriage to him and being subservient to him would have been another in her string of doing at best *okay* in things because she didn't care enough and wasn't confident enough to do more. Like everything else. Until that moment well over a year earlier, she never would have broken it off. She was—now—glad she had.

After lunch on Thursday, Evelyn drove her BMW to get food at the town's overpriced grocery store. She avoided the wide selection of prepared meals and wandered up-and-down the aisles. *What can I make? What can I make for Bridget?* Bridget had done the cooking on Tuesday and Wednesday. Nothing fancy but Evelyn enjoyed it and enjoyed helping.

Up-and-down the aisles. Pushing her little cart. Finally, she decided that even she, a master of the microwave and take out dinners, could probably make burgers. Ground beef, buns, frozen fries. Can of baked beans. She was excited when she proudly entered the house with her two grocery bags.

It was about four and after she put the things in the kitchen, she lightly tapped on the den's door. That room was hardly an example of the darkness one associates with the word. Instead, it had a large window that looked out to the east and instead of being covered by wooden panels, its walls were cream colored and decorated with a set of watercolors of beach scenes, hung so that each naturally flowed into the next one.

The furniture was simple and nice and comfortable.

To Evelyn, the presence of Bridget at the desk with her single monitor, it was also very, very inviting. When she was told to come in, she entered with two glasses of Chardonnay and was met by a warm smile from the woman to whom the second glass was intended.

Evelyn plopped down onto a chair and asked what Bridget was working on. Bridget took a long sip and placed the glass on her desk. She had told Evelyn about the Foundation. She rotated her chair and provided details to the sketches she'd given about Peter and Amy and Petey in their prior conversations. Now she focused on the specifics of the Foundation. Evelyn was surprised that she found it interesting. A glimpse into the world of a business with which she was unfamiliar in her nondescript department at Chase.

After a few minutes, Bridget paused and said, "I'm sorry to bore you." Evelyn denied, truthfully, being bored and asked if she could get her book and just sit while Bridget worked. "I promise to keep quiet." Bridget found this oddly endearing and relented. It would be nice to have some company while she reviewed some grant proposals.

For the rest of the afternoon, the two sat in their own worlds together, Bridget at her desk and Evelyn sprawled across the loveseat. Both liked it. After which Evelyn made her dinner. The night ended with a Rom-Com on Netflix that the two had both seen more than once. That didn't matter, though, to how much they enjoyed it, exchanging snarky comments throughout.

On Friday, Bridget took the day off. She got what she needed to do finished and thought it would be fun to spend the entire day with Evelyn. Things would change dramatically with the coming of Peter, Amy, and Petey late in the day and, probably, Fran, Jane, and Eve in the morning. They went for a drive after Evelyn showered following her six-mile run—five miles on the roads and a final gut-wrenching mile along the beach—chatting and laughing, laughing and chatting. They got a couple of salads in town and drove home. For the first time that week, they used the pool.

Bridget was shocked. Evelyn was wearing a poured-into—Bridget thought it could have been porned-into it was so *hot*—one-piece and Bridget found herself staring. Just for a moment, but she felt guilty for objectifying her friend as she had been objectified her entire life. Evelyn sensed it but put Bridget at ease with a dive and a beckoning for Bridget to join her in the water. Then they swam back and forth a bit before holding themselves up by their arms in the deep end to talk.

This time, the talk was more serious than it was in recent days. Their time alone was coming to an end and seriousness would close the circle that began with that first, random conversation on the beach.

"I've never met someone who has done what you have for me. Just by letting me talk," Evelyn said.

Bridget elbowed the taller woman and said, "I can't tell you how happy I am for having met you." Their eyes locked, for a moment, before Evelyn pushed away with her upper arms and did a few more laps before hoisting herself over the side and grabbing a towel to sit on a chaise. Bridget used the ladder to get out.

3.

"HE'S JUST A regular guy. He just happens to be really, really rich. And not asshole rich."

If Bridget said it once, she said it a dozen times. Evelyn didn't quite believe it. Not the rich part. The other. She sure as hell wouldn't be *regular* if she had his boatload of cash.

"You'll see" and a shrug was what Bridget ended up with. "You'll see."

It was a bit after six and more than once Evelyn thought her little Cinderella story was coming to a close, and it might be best to simply head over to her share and get on with things and she might have done that if Bridget didn't say she at least had to thank the Edgars for allowing her to stay.

Amy texted when they got off the LIE, the dreaded Long Island Expressway. Bridget and Evelyn had dinner ready. Nothing fancy. But after Bridget complained that Evelyn's burger was so raw "I think I heard a 'moo' when I bit into it," Evelyn was leaving the principal cooking to Bridget, happy to make the salad.

The Porsche SUV pulled in at about 6:10. Peter driving and Amy with Petey in the back. Peter and Amy knew of Evelyn from Bridget's reports. He shook her hand and she gave her a hug and a "welcome." They seemed nice enough with their toddler.

And this and what Bridget had told her were at odds with the conventional wisdom she had long held that Peter Edgar was a filthy rich cad and bastard and borderline abuser who seduced and knocked up and then abandoned an innocent nurse and then bought her off with some of his pocket change.

That conviction had been eroded in her time with Bridget and the easy and admiring way she spoke of Peter. And was now almost gone when she actually met him and his wife and son.

Having let that prejudice fade, Evelyn actually enjoyed the weekend. It was, after all, like a palatial retreat. And she met that supposedly innocent nurse on Saturday morning when she showed up with her baby and her mother and her mother's boyfriend.

That boyfriend was called Todd Newman. He seemed nice enough. Maybe ten years younger than Jane. 5' 11" or so with short hair and well-defined pecs and a flat stomach. He was an electrician who had always been good with his hands. He'd met Jane when doing work at Jane's Manhattan law firm. After some flirting on site, they got together when the job was done and it grew until they became an item.

As soon as she met him, though, Evelyn sensed something sleazy about him. She well knew that particular feeling from her sometimes sordid past and she told herself to be careful. Hook-ups with guys like that almost never ended well.

Bridget and to some extent Amy picked up on this too and they immediately felt protective about Jane, who clearly didn't see it, and Fran, who was doing her best to ignore it if she did.

Later that day, Evelyn, Bridget, and Amy walked into town with Petey in a stroller for a walk, giving some dad-time for Peter with Eve and Fran and to give Jane and Todd some of their own alone-time.

After about an hour, Petey nodded off. Evelyn had learned more about Amy. Not as sweet as Bridget. But shy and considerate in her own way.

As to Fran, Evelyn paid attention when they got back, and it was clear how much Fran adored Eve. She did not, though, seem to be the damsel who was the victim Evelyn thought she was before meeting everyone, although there was tension between the Fran Camp and the Peter Camp. That was undeniable, and Bridget had warned her about it. The rough edges had been smoothed by time. They were still there though.

A large Saturday dinner on the deck went well.

At dusk, Peter asked if anyone wanted to go into the pool. Evelyn saw Todd glance at her. She ignored it and rose, saying she would get her suit. Bridget whispered to Amy, "You better keep your eye on him," nodding towards Peter, "I've seen what she looks like in a bathing suit." Amy nodded. She knew Peter would look, more than he should, but he was in no danger: If the red-carpet women didn't get him, another beauty wouldn't.

Jane decided to stay out on the deck and not sit by the pool with the others.

In the end, Evelyn didn't make it into the pool either. When she got undressed to put on her suit, she decided she didn't want to be displayed before strangers, as she unavoidably would be. That had never bothered her before. In fact, she'd relished it, even the teasing she directed at men. It was mean, but she thrilled at causing *excitement* in a tight bathing suit of a twenty- or thirty-something guy.

She didn't know why, but suddenly the thought bothered her. So, she put her shorts and T-shirt back on and sat in a chaise lounge at the side of the pool, watching the others. When she got up to get a refill, Evelyn noticed Jane sat alone on the deck, away from the pool, and she sat near her. Both women were shy with strangers and both women were strangers. It was enough that they simply sat quietly next to each other, staring out over the dunes to the waves.

"I met Bridget on the beach," Evelyn said.

"So I hear."

"What do you think of her?" Evelyn asked.

"I barely know her. I have enough trouble getting comfortable with Peter and Amy. She seems very nice from what I've seen. And she and my Fran go way back."

Which is where the conversation ended. The two sat in awkward silence, listening to the waves and hearing the shouts from the pool over to the right.

As she sat and reflected, Evelyn was happy, replaying the week in her brain and sad that it would soon be over, the clock will have struck midnight, and she would be back to her nondescript job and nondescript world. She turned in early to finish her book.

About thirty minutes after she went to her room, Evelyn heard a light rapping on her door. She was still up and reading in bed.

"Come in."

It was Bridget. Evelyn put the book aside after marking the page. Bridget sat on the bed.

"Things will get a bit crazy tomorrow when everyone leaves so I wanted to talk. How do you feel?"

"I feel that the woman who you saw on the beach was washed away." She threw her hands up and away with a smile. She couldn't help it, but Evelyn suddenly began to cry. "I can't thank—"

Bridget stopped her by leaning over to put her arm around her. This woman wasn't nearly as fucked-up as she had been on Monday. "You know," Bridget said, "you're so much better than that woman. I've seen that this week. Promise you'll be my friend."

Evelyn couldn't help but smile. "I promise." With that Bridget ran her fingers along the other's cheek.

"Good. I'd like that." And she left Evelyn to finish her novel, which she did quickly through the happy denouement of a story of true love prevailing. A fairy tale, perhaps, but a nice story in the end.

After a final lunch the next day on the deck and quick goodbyes and thanks to everyone and a precious hug from Bridget by the BMW's open door, Evelyn drove from the circular drive and headed west, hoping she'd gotten started early enough to beat the traffic and be at her own apartment early enough to get ready for work on the dreaded first-day-back Monday.

She was surprised on Tuesday morning when Bridget called and said that instead of going to that shared house for the rest of the month, she was welcome to *slum it* at Peter and Amy's. Without a moment of hesitation, she accepted the offer.

"I've vouched for you," Bridget said and one of the guest rooms unofficially became Evelyn's. There were, after all, plenty to go around.

4

WHEN HER *VACATION* (or whatever it was) ended, Bridget was back in the city. Now that Peter and Amy had established themselves as a married couple with a toddler, she usually stayed in the apartment instead of going all the way to Woodlawn. It was a little over a mile and on pleasant days, she enjoyed the walk to and from work, as Amy had when she was at Enswich & Taylor.

About that, Amy had returned six months after Petey appeared on the scene, generally working remotely from the apartment. Peter wondered that it took her that long to realize that she wasn't cut out to be an Upper East Side Lady Who Lunched.

With Petey left in the good hands of a live-in nanny during the day, Amy resumed her walking to her office at 40th and Madison and lunching on a salad and iced tea or coffee from the place on Fifth with Sarah and others from the office.

When Bridget stayed over at the apartment, she joined Amy and the two made a habit when not window-shopping-on-the-fly of Madison Avenue boutiques of heading to the west and walking down the southern stretches of Central Park past the boat pond and the *Alice in Wonderland* sculpture that kids played on and through the Zoo where they often brought Petey. Quite by accident and quite inevitably they evolved into becoming best friends.

In the rain, they shared an Uber, which was not nearly as much fun.

Bridget made sure to be at the condo on Thursday nights. Once a month or so, Peter and Amy would get all dressed up and Amy would select among the couture gowns Peter insisted be made for her to a benefit or gala at one of the elite ballrooms scattered about Manhattan. And always, always, the dazzling diamond bracelet that had been Peter's father's gift to his mother was on Amy's left wrist. In time, it became second nature for her to run her finger across the initials CE that were engraved on its clasp and thought it horribly sad that Michael and Carly Edgar would never meet and hold their grandson.

Amy had long since understood the theatrical part of these events and slipped gracefully and very well-dressed into their superficiality, as was and always had been the nature of elite New York society.

As for Page Six and *The Times*'s Society Page and the ever increasing number of fashionista blogs and Insta streams, they had long since moved on from Peter Edgar, there being little interest and less of a market for the goings-on and goings-about of a handsome, rich married father of a toddler.

For her part, Bridget made a point of calling Evelyn every few nights. At first, it was checking in. But soon the calls lost their therapeutic character and became longer and more spontaneous. They met for lunch now and then and before either knew it, they were…friends, with Amy sometimes joining them for lunch or shopping excursions.

The "new" Evelyn didn't go unnoticed at work. Her boss, Dorothy Watkins, increased her responsibilities and Evelyn learned her department wasn't as nondescript as she had long thought it. She didn't *enjoy* it yet. But she began to dislike it less.

5.

IN LATE AUGUST, the dog days of summer, things were crawling along at Chase for Evelyn. On Thursday night, she received a call from "Todd. You know. Jane's friend." She didn't know how he'd gotten her number but they'd established a kind of rapport on the weekends when they were both at the East Hampton house, though Todd largely ignored her in favor of Jane. Evelyn's initial caution about him had relaxed.

In the call, Todd said Peter had asked him to do some work on the house. He wondered whether Evelyn would keep him company and give him a ride out in the morning in her fancy BMW. His own truck was in the shop, he said, and Jane, Fran, and Eve weren't going out until Saturday and he owed it to Peter to take care of it ASAP.

It was all innocent enough and since work at her back-office job was in its doldrums period anyway, she took a personal day and told Bridget she was heading out early and would see her when she arrived later on Friday when she would show up with Amy and the others.

She neglected to mention Todd.

It was a fun ride out. Traffic was light and they made good time. They stopped at a casual open-air restaurant a few miles west of East Hampton. Todd was relaxed and charming. Asking about her. Letting her tease him about some coleslaw that was stuck on his upper lip when they were having their tuna sandwiches and Cokes in the open air at the café on Route 27 and then letting her reach over to remove it, her fingers and their eyes lingering a beat longer than necessary.

By the time they reached the house and Todd had unlocked the door and turned off the alarm, Evelyn *wanted* him. It was mutual. They both knew it. She didn't care about anyone or anything else. It had been a while and she just needed a man to be inside her and he was ready, willing, and, she hoped, able. It didn't hurt that she had noticed his pecs and his abs and a number of other things a woman, especially a horny one, notices in a man.

In the foyer and its pine floors with its view across the great room and out to the Atlantic, he turned and put his arms around her, standing at the open door.

"You are so fuckin' beautiful." It was his growl in her right ear and she was more deeply excited.

They kissed for the first time. After it was done and the tongues released and the breaths caught, nothing mattered to her but getting on her back so he could enter her.

She raced ahead of him up the stairs, unbuttoning her blouse as she did. They went into the large master bedroom. That was the perfect, indeed the only, place for this. She'd never been taken to or on a bed anywhere nearly as nice as this. They would have plenty of time to tidy up. *No one would know. Why not?*

Between entering the bedroom and getting to the bed, all of her clothes and underwear and her shoes were off, thrown in a pile to the right. He, too, was rapidly getting his things off, though pausing to take out a condom package that *happened* to be in his jeans. She saw it and said not to bother, that she was on the pill. Which was true but she also wanted nothing between them when he entered her.

Evelyn ripped the fluffy duvet aside and lay in the middle of the large bed. She looked at him and he looked big. Sweat and arousal oozing from him. A man. She spread her legs. No foreplay. She was ready and he was hard. He placed his legs between hers and their eyes met as she reached and directed him. It went in so smoothly.

It had been so long. Not since that asshole banker in an Escalade parked on a dead end a couple of days before Bridget had rescued her on the beach. That was a hook-up.

This? This was glorious. Her mind cleared of everything but the feel of this man filling her. She was rocking and moaning in time with his movement and thrusts and then she came. Loudly. Very loudly since there was no one nearby who could hear her.

Evelyn didn't know that Bridget unexpectedly had left the city at about lunchtime to surprise her friend. After she'd gotten Evelyn's message, she decided it'd be a hoot to just show up and the two of them could just hang out on the deck or on the beach with no one else, like they'd done that first week together. She Ubered to the Bronx to get her dad's Toyota and got on the road early enough to beat the summer deluge of traffic heading to the Hamptons.

When she got to the house, Evelyn's BMW was parked in front. She used her key and noticed that the alarm wasn't set. She didn't see Evelyn in the great room or out on the deck. She didn't hear her in the kitchen. It was clear to Bridget that her friend was on the beach and Bridget could change into something appropriate and go down and find her.

She was at the bottom of the stairs when she heard noises coming from above, echoing down to the great room. She wasn't so naïve that she didn't recognize the sound. Two people were fucking. She recognized Evelyn's voice—moaning desperately—and then a *Come On Baby* she realized was from Todd. Jane's Todd.

Bridget turned to escape, not as a question of privacy but as one of abject disgust. As she stepped back down the stairs, she heard Evelyn's shouted *I'm coming* as she did. Then Todd's *Come for me, bitch,* she slowly reversed her steps and hurried through the foyer as quickly and quietly as she could to get as far from the disgusting betrayal she'd had the great misfortune of happening upon.

But it was not quiet enough. As Todd was reaching his own climax, Evelyn heard tires on the pebbles out front. Her sudden ecstasy disappeared in a flash and she pushed the yet-to-come Todd off of her and to the side. She reached the window just in time to see that the driver was Bridget and to watch the car disappear down Peter's street.

It hit her like a bolt of lightning. She panicked at realizing she'd been discovered doing what she'd been doing with Jane's boyfriend but this was a thousand times worse. Because she realized out-of-the-blue that Bridget, Bridget Casey, was the last person in the world she wanted to discover her lewd and deceitful act.

Todd couldn't care less. "What about me?" he asked as she stood frozen and helpless at the window. "I'm so close."

Evelyn turned to him and said that Bridget had discovered them and that she didn't give a fuck whether he came or not. Todd laid there looking somewhat ridiculous as he lightly stroked his dick while she vanished from the room.

She came back carrying a stack of clean sheets she'd collected from the linen closet down the hall. She looked at him.

"Just get up and dressed for Christ's sake."

"But what about me?"

Evelyn turned, her face crimson, "Fuck you, asshole. Don't you know what we've done?"

"Way to ruin the mood," he called to her glorious naked back and he didn't bother finishing.

"You're a pitiful shit," she told him. He got out of the bed and dressed.

A shit just like me, Evelyn told herself as she battled to control the tears of regret and sorrow for what she had done and what she may have thrown away by doing it. She got dressed too and together they were able to make the bed and she found a hamper into which to place the *evidence.*

An hour later, Evelyn Manners was alone, heading west on the LIE returning to the city with the music blaring to try to drown out whatever it was she was feeling.

Todd had remained behind. He really had promised Peter that he'd take care of something in the house and he was happy not to be sitting alone with the stuck-up bitch for two hours. So was she.

If Todd didn't care, Evelyn did nothing but care. When she recognized Bridget in the car, it had been a revelation. Bridget was the one person who she didn't want to know what she'd done. Which was, to put it bluntly but accurately, fucking another woman's boyfriend.

The epiphany that she cared so much because she may have fallen in love with Bridget washed over her. Evelyn had never given a conscious thought to the blonde nurse in that way.

And now that she did, Bridget was gone. She had never felt anything like this emptiness before about anyone.

Bridget, she knew, wasn't gone because Evelyn had cheated on *her*. She was gone because she had cheated on Jane. Which, it necessarily followed, made her unworthy of Bridget's own love. If Bridget had ever given any thought in that direction towards Evelyn.

As she drove to the city, Evelyn found herself reliving that morning when she sat on the beach in July. In the damp and under a clearing sky. It was a now treasured memory, the most treasured of all her life and that memory was all she still had. The beautiful, wonderful woman touching her arm and asking to hear what Evelyn had to say. Bridget was Evelyn's first *friend*. The first to see through the curse that was the taller woman's beauty.

And now she'd witnessed how empty and evil that beauty proved to be.

6.

WHILE SHE THOUGHT EVELYN and Todd were still doing whatever they were doing at the house, Bridget sat outside the Starbucks on Main Street in East Hampton. She figured in an hour they'd either be gone or would've made the place presentable/nothing-to-see-here. They'd been none the wiser about her surprise appearance and quick retreat and were probably lying in post-coital bliss in the lush bed clothes of Peter and Amy's bedroom. She wondered bitterly whether they'd set an alarm to make sure they'd made the place presentable before the owners showed up.

That thought kept her slightly amused for only a moment before she returned to the complexities of what she'd just witnessed.

What could she do?
Who could she tell?
Who should she tell?
Peter?
Amy?
Jane?

She felt a weight. Part of her believed she'd heard nothing but the sounds of two animals copulating. Mating.

Then, out of nowhere, Bridget felt something entirely unexpected and foreign to her. It was the full force of an emotion that had never even grazed her before.

Jealousy.

She wanted to be on that bed. Not Evelyn. Todd. She wanted to be Todd. She wanted to be the one to make Evelyn come. She wanted to be the one who made Evelyn scream.

The fact, though, was that Bridget was a virgin. She had *desires.* She was not asexual. Up in Woodlawn she'd dated, mostly guys from the neighborhood. Cops and firemen and guys in the trades from Dublin or Galway or some farm in County Limerick.

Many, perhaps most, of them tried to get into her pants, but she'd resisted. Not from any *saving myself* BS but because, yes, she was a romantic and she wanted the first time to be worth it. And none of the guys she'd dated, even guys she'd gone out with three or four times, seemed worth it however excitedly they tried.

That she suddenly felt something special about another woman was disturbing to her. But it was also undeniable. The thought seemed natural and unnatural at the same time. Troubling yet strangely liberating.

And the irony was that now that she'd suddenly discovered this possible inclination in her heart, she knew that the woman who triggered it would never think that way towards her. Evelyn's obvious straight orientation was on full display less than an hour before.

A sad irony indeed.

The Starbucks air suddenly became suffocating. Bridget grabbed her cup and stormed out onto the sidewalk, bumping against a couple as she did. After apologizing, she knew enough not to get into her car. Her brain was in no shape to allow her to drive. She would just walk to the house and on the way try to prepare herself for what she expected to find when she got there.

If they were still there, fuck it. With each stride, she got angrier and angrier. *Fuck 'em all.* She knew what they all thought of her, not unkindly. *Bridget will take care of everything. Bridget is so fucking sweet. CALL 1-800-BRIDGET! Bridget is the type who would comfort a stranger on the beach.* Bridget saw all these small, empty beds where kids slept their last. It was the bubbling up of an emotional turmoil that she always kept within herself. She stopped. It erupted.

"FUCK THEM ALL."

She nearly screamed it into the quiet Hamptons night.

She neared the house. Evelyn's car was gone. She had her keys as she stepped onto the front step and was about to go in when she saw Todd, visible through the window by the front door. There he was, sitting on the deck, with an early afternoon drink and staring out over the Atlantic like Jay Gatsby. The smug asshole.

He didn't see her, and she scooted well to the side of the house where the path led to the beach, and she went down to the spot where she had first seen and then comforted Evelyn.

It was a feeling she'd never known about a man let alone about a woman. Now for the first time in her life, she felt an ache to have someone make honest love to her. To feel the physical connection and to feel physical passion with another human being. And it was a woman, a particular woman, she craved.

She lowered herself down where she had that Monday in July, though thankfully the sand was dry this time. Suddenly she couldn't get the phrase *That Day* out of her mind.

That Day. It changed so much for Evelyn. *But could it have changed everything for her as well? Does fate work that way in real life?*

Bridget turned. She could see the window in the master bedroom. Where the woman she'd suddenly discovered she loved was with someone who was not her, being noisily ecstatic with someone who wasn't Bridget Casey.

She turned back to the ocean, watching the waves just as Evelyn did *That Day*. Suddenly lost and confused, wondering what had become of her life. It had gone on without her. And now Evelyn was gone without her.

Bridget was brought back to the present when her phone pinged.

{Evelyn:} I need to speak to you. Please call. E.

She didn't know why Evelyn was asking this. She didn't know that Evelyn knew Bridget had caught the fucking. She only knew that she had driven off who knows where and that she couldn't talk to her. Not yet at least. Maybe later. But not now. She ignored the text.

She got up and brushed her shorts off and headed to the house. It was nearly five. Peter, Amy, and Petey would arrive in a few hours. Fran, Eve, and Jane would be coming in the morning, and Bridget felt a chill about that.

And Todd. He was already there.

What about Evelyn, wherever she was? She'd be back eventually and Bridget needed time to compose herself when they finally saw each other but she'd cross that bridge when she got to it.

When she was inside, Bridget went to the door to the deck and exchanged a *hello* with Todd, still lazily looking out to the ocean. She noticed he gave her something of a confused look but assumed that was simply for her arriving without the others, and she gave no indication that she knew something about him other than the usual. She otherwise tried to ignore him.

Bridget went to her room and slipped down the hall for a peek at the master bedroom. It looked presentable but she recognized that the bed had been made haphazardly, something the cleaning crew that came every Tuesday would never have allowed.

She returned downstairs. Todd was still sunning on the deck. It was early but Bridget desperately needed a drink. Without asking Todd if he wanted anything, she made a gin & tonic for herself. Instead of sitting out on the deck, she went to the side of the house and pulled up a beach lounge by the pool and sat there. From where she sat, she would hear Peter's car and she could think about what she was going to do and how she was going to react when they got there.

She'd just gotten settled when her phone pinged again. She saw it was another text from Evelyn. She read it.

> *{Evelyn:} I KNOW YOU WERE THERE. I NEED TO SPEAK TO YOU. PLEASE CALL ME. I NEED TO SPEAK TO YOU.*

I know you were there? This surprised Bridget. It meant that Evelyn knew Bridget had caught them. *How?* The how didn't matter. She stared at her phone in her left hand, swirling the ice in the glass in her right. She thought of Evelyn and if nothing else she recognized the All Caps as some sort of call for...something. She hit her number. It answered before the second ring.

Evelyn was crying.

"Bridget. I need to see you. I need to see you and explain."

"About what?" This was crueler than Bridget normally imagined she could be but she could not help herself as her anger bubbled back up.

"You know about what. I'm begging you. I'm back in the city but when I got home I realized I needed to see you."

"Why?"

"Please, Bridget. I can't do this over the phone. I can be in East Hampton in a couple of hours. Please tell me you'll meet me. Please."

Bridget's emotions were bouncing everywhere. She thought she knew why Evelyn *needed to see* her. It was pretty clear that she wanted to limit the damage, convince Bridget to keep the secret. If possible, salvage whatever friendship they had. And especially keep what access she had to Peter and his house and other perks.

Bridget would be right to just tell Peter and Amy when they arrived. Consequences. Let them figure out what to do. Be done with it. Be done with her.

This thought immediately cascaded through Bridget's mind but she couldn't do this to the woman she now realized she loved.

"Alright," she finally said. "I won't say anything till I speak to you. Send me a text when you get off the LIE. Traffic will be bad, but I'll meet you at the Starbucks on Main. I'll make my excuses to everyone."

"Thank you, Bridget, thank you." Even over the phone Bridget could hear her relief.

7

TWO HOURS LATER, Evelyn's status text to Bridget finally arrived. She reported that she'd reached Route 27, which on a Friday would get her to East Hampton in about thirty minutes. There was plenty of time to walk back into town for her rendezvous with Evelyn. She told Peter and Amy that Evelyn wanted to meet her. When Amy asked, "what's up?," Bridget simply said she wasn't sure.

In fact, Bridget wasn't sure. She wasn't nearly as angry at the world as she retraced her steps, in reverse, from earlier. More than anything she was confused, desperate to hear what Evelyn was going to say. She didn't know whether Evelyn had any feelings towards her let alone feelings of the sort that were coursing through her veins and, given what she'd heard earlier that day, she very much doubted it. She had agreed to meet with Evelyn, though, and that's what she was going to do even if it was the last time they would ever meet. And this final thought saddened her. But that was out of her control.

The brief phone conversation with Evelyn in some ways calmed Bridget but it also made her anxious. She sat at her little round table on the sidewalk as couples and groups from the city mingled past, chattering excitedly about the beginning of a weekend in town and the beaches where they'd lie and the parties they'd attend and hookups they'd try to enjoy.

The image of young people enjoying free and uncomplicated sex in this glittering capital of New York wealth saddened her too. She was not built that way. Many of the nurses she used to work with used sex as a release from all the stress they endured day-after-day on the wards, primal stress of the sort these financial whizzes and lawyers could not imagine. Fran was one of them but Bridget didn't envy that. She understood it, but it just wasn't something she had an interest in doing.

And now she imagined how liberating it would be to just lay down with another human being—in her case a particular human being—and perform her own basic, primal act.

She shook her head and took more of her coffee. The sounds of passersby returned as she focused on the task at hand.

She was back in the moment. Her eyes kept flickering to the west. Evelyn's BMW would be coming from that direction. And then she saw it, slowing along the row of parked cars, looking for a spot.

A black Mercedes SUV was pulling out two or three shops away, and Evelyn slowed to take the space. As the car backed in, Bridget gathered her napkin and cup and headed towards it. In contrast to Bridget's jeans and T-shirt and loosely dropping hair, Evelyn was in her typical, seemingly effortless outfit of neat black slacks with a cream blouse tucked in. Her hair though, was in a messy ponytail and not the carefully tended bob she usually had.

By the time Evelyn had gotten out and locked the car, Bridget was standing right there on the sidewalk. Evelyn stopped between cars when she saw Bridget. She took a deep breath. She'd been rehearsing this moment ever since Bridget had agreed to meet her. She went to her.

Her heart collapsed before she could get a word out. Bridget was glaring at her.

"Well?"

All of the inadequate words that Evelyn had practiced on the drive vanished. Still, she was able to hold back the tears, her supply of them having been exhausted in the hours since she knew Bridget had *heard*. She instead let her heart do the talking. She thought of extending her arms, but Bridget had crossed hers. Evelyn crossed hers, but not the way Bridget had. For her, her fingers interlaced to try to give her some stability in her pose. She nodded.

"I love you and I fucked it all up."

Bridget was not prepared for this revelation and she let her arms drop to her sides. Evelyn's tears began. Her words became choppy. "Tell me you can forgive me. Tell me what I need to do for you to forgive me."

Bridget was stunned and had no idea what to do or say. Evelyn was not gay. Hell, she was in bed with a man only hours before.

Evelyn's face dropped, looking to the sidewalk as her shoulders heaved. People passing by were looking at the couple, wondering what was going on but quickly returning to their own worlds. Without thinking, Bridget put her arms around Evelyn. She pulled her tight, feeling the heaving of the broken, lost woman who'd just come out to her. *To her.* For the first time since that day when they met, she looked like that same lost woman on the beach. All the calm she had witnessed growing was gone.

"I want you to want me to love you," Evelyn said, as she pushed away.

Both women hated what was happening and the path that had led them to it. Evelyn didn't want to be treated like that lost child anymore, and Bridget didn't want to be a caretaker. As she was being held, Evelyn heard the slight whisper, "I love you, too" from Bridget. Bridget didn't mean to say it but didn't regret the words. She repeated them. Evelyn caught her breath and stopped shuttering.

The two separated, only their hands being connected.

Still, Bridget could not comprehend what Evelyn had just said given all that had happened. She had to be clear. "When you say love me," she asked, "you mean something more than as friends?"

"Yes. Way more. Do you?"

Honesty and hope deserved honesty and hope.

"Yes," Bridget said, and Evelyn's face was transformed into something unimaginably beautiful.

Bridget wondered whether Evelyn could see the improvement in her own face, which she at least knew was there. She suggested they walk in the clear, cooling air.

They headed away from the stores and restaurants and the beautiful people crowding the sidewalk on the fine evening. Soon they were in a quiet area of grand houses with expansive lawns set back well off the street and behind tall privet hedges. Expensive cars and SUVs meandered by them as they walked in the street, gradually and perhaps unconsciously leaning against each other as the lovers each very much wanted to become.

Keeping her voice low in the quiet street beneath a canopy of century old elms, Bridget said, "I'll listen to whatever you want to say to me."

Evelyn really didn't know how to explain. She was left simply to tell Bridget the truth as far as she understood it.

It was fun driving out with Todd. It was wrong. She of course knew it was wrong in so many ways but she couldn't help flirting with him. She was not putting responsibility for this on anyone but herself. She had no one to blame but Evelyn Manners. Full stop.

By the time they neared East Hampton, she was thinking what it would be like to go to bed with a man, any man. It had been so long. As they drove to the house, she became more and more relaxed with him. Older and in very good shape. Sure, a bit full of himself. That, she told herself, didn't matter. What mattered is that he was sexy and she was attracted to him. And he was a man with all that meant and it had been way too long since she'd opened her legs for one.

By then, there was no Jane, if only in her excited brain. Todd was just a strong, handsome man.

He wasn't very adept at seduction. He thought he had this whole macho-thing that would work. It didn't. Evelyn needed no seduction. She needed to be fucked and she needed a man to fuck her.

He was above her, but she was fucking him more than he was fucking her. While they were doing it, she didn't give a shit about anything, or anyone. She kept on the pill even though she hadn't had sex for a while. Just in case. It was good. The sex with Todd was good.

"Then as I was coming down from my orgasm," she said, "I heard tires. I threw him off of me and ran to the window. It's then that I realized who it was that had caught us and why you were leaving."

She said that the moment she saw Bridget and understood that Bridget must have witnessed at least some of what was going on in the master bedroom, and surely enough to know of her betrayal, a strange feeling came over her. Now she cared. Not the least about the naked, now frustrated man in Peter and Amy's bed. She cared that it was Bridget and her world came together and exploded at the same moment.

She knew she had to confess. "I didn't realize it, that I love you, until I saw you drive away and knew that I had lost you before I'd ever really had you. As a woman. As a mate. Until that moment, I never thought of you, or any woman, like that. Just being with you. I loved that day when you let me just sit with you while you were working."

Bridget remained quiet. Evelyn waited. *Why wouldn't she respond?* Finally, Bridget too confessed.

"And I loved that first day too. I've loved every day I've been with you. I didn't realize how much till today. Until I heard you being so intimate with someone else. Hearing how excited you were with Todd. It didn't matter in that moment that it was with a man. What mattered is that it was not with me."

She exhaled, letting the visceral heat from that memory cool. They could not pretend that the betrayal didn't happen. Neither knew what to do to at least have the prospect of them moving forward as a couple, the irony, of course, being that but for the betrayal these mutual feelings for one another would never have come to the surface.

Evelyn was trying to process the words that flowed over her.

Bridget stopped and turned, and Evelyn did the same.

"I never thought of you, or any woman, like that either. Never. Then I thought of how much I wanted to just...make love to you."

With that hanging in the air, they resumed walking, their hands tightening their grips. "I hated you because I wanted you, but you were doing this horrible thing to Jane. How could you? How do we get over that?"

Evelyn's voice was broken. She didn't know the answer.

"I need you to know I've been with a lot of men," she began. "But I promise you I've never done anything like that before. Ever. I swear. I wouldn't sleep with a guy if I knew he had a girlfriend. Sometimes I didn't know, and it made me feel like shit when I found out he'd lied to me. What I did to the other woman. But I didn't know who she was. I fucking know who Jane is."

They stopped and again faced one another.

"Bridget, I have no excuse or explanation for what I did except I needed to get laid. It wasn't his fault. He may have hoped it would happen when we left the city. But I was the one who flirted with him. Double *entendres*. Laughing at his jokes. Clearing mayo from his lips. That's on me. I've no excuse."

"You betrayed Jane. You know that?"

"I'll always know that I betrayed her. Always. It's the worst thing I've ever done in my miserable life."

Bridget wasn't letting Evelyn go the pity route.

"Stop with the bullshit about your *miserable life*. That was then. This is now. This was this afternoon for God's sake."

Evelyn was taken aback at this onslaught from a woman who just said she loved her. Now she was the silent one. They resumed their walk and reached a corner and turned back into town. The trees created a tunnel toward Route 27. Evelyn waited for a car to pass. She stopped again.

"You're right." Evelyn's face dropped to look at the road beneath her feet. "I'm not who I was. I'm not going to tell you I'm *worse*. I might be, but that doesn't matter. What matters is what I do and whether what I do matters to you."

They were walking again.

"Evie. Love. This may sound horrible." Evelyn tensed at Bridget's words. "I know that's not who you are. I know you are the person who's going to sit down with Jane and tell her what happened. I can't say what Jane will do about it. I can't say whether she'll forgive you. Or that Fran will.

"If you do that, *I* will forgive you. If you do that, I will not abandon you. You fucked up. I'm not doing this for you. I'm doing this for me. I want to be with the woman who you are. I'm doing this for me."

With that, the two continued their walk in silence. Bridget convinced Evelyn to go to the house. She said she thought Jane would arrive in the morning with Fran and Eve.

Todd was there already—explaining that a friend had given him a lift—but he and Evelyn stayed well clear of each other. Bridget said she told Peter and Amy she was meeting her but didn't say what it was about. When they got to the house, she'd tell them that things were okay. She'd leave it to Jane to say more.

Evelyn got to her car first and headed toward Peter and Amy's place. She waited by the side of the road for Bridget to go by.

Bridget passed a minute later and the two entered the driveway and then the house together. They both gave great performances. Neither Peter nor Amy noticed a change in them. Todd was still sitting out by the pool, away from Evelyn.

8.

THEY DIDN'T SLEEP MUCH, Bridget and Evelyn. Both were awake when the dawn began to lighten the house up and they both listened to the deep quiet of the sleeping house, exaggerating the familiar rhythmic sound of the waves lapping against the beach.

Neither dared get up lest she meet the other until Bridget heard Evelyn use the hall bathroom and then her scurrying back to her room, the clicking of the closing door echoing like a shot.

Bridget took advantage and used the bathroom herself. Before she returned to her room, she went to Evelyn's door and knocked lightly.

"I know you're up."

A moment later, Evelyn opened the door. She stood there with her hair a mess and her eyes reddened in nothing but an oversized Horace Greely High School T-shirt she usually wore when she was at the house. Bridget had glanced at herself in the bathroom mirror and knew she wasn't much more presentable.

Evelyn stepped aside and Bridget went in. They sat beside each other on the bed and without thinking held hands.

"I didn't sleep," Bridget said.

"Neither did I."

With a squeeze of Evelyn's hand, Bridget got up. "I love you," she said in almost a whisper, "and I'll be there for you on the other side."

Evelyn nodded with a hint of a desperate smile and watched the woman she loved open and go through her door back to her room. She waited and tried to get back asleep, it being too early to wake the house up by going downstairs. And she did drift off and was awakened by the sounds of a new morning, particularly the crying of Petey from somewhere downstairs.

When Evelyn reached the kitchen itself, she saw Bridget out on the deck, the deck where they'd spent so many happy hours during their glorious first week together. The thought sent a chill through her. *Would they ever have such a moment again?*

Before she could get a cup of the coffee from the carafe, Bridget came in. She stood beside Evelyn as she put her mug into the sink for cleaning. She looked to see if anyone was watching and with the coast clear she ran a finger across Evelyn's hand on the counter.

She passed by and said she was heading out for a bike ride. No one offered to go with her. An hour later, Evelyn herself was out of the house. She had slathered herself in sunscreen and tightened her hair's ponytail and went on her normal Saturday morning run although this Saturday was anything but *normal.*

When she was gone, Amy said to Peter, "What is going on with those two?"

"I have no idea," he said, "but it's definitely something."

"We'll just have to see. But they're not together this morning. Something's going to blow. I just hope it happens soon so everyone can relax."

"Or at least recover."

The couple resumed what they were doing, which chiefly consisted of taking care of Petey and wondering whether Bridget and Evelyn had had a fight, which would be strange since they always got on so well with one another.

The next thing the morning brought was Fran, Eve, and Jane. Todd had come down when Evelyn had left for her run and greeted the newcomers when they arrived.

Bridget and Evelyn made sure to be gone when they did. Bridget got back about twenty minutes after they arrived. She tried to be her typical self with them, but Fran and Jane both noticed she was tense.

Evelyn returned about fifteen minutes later. She was covered in sweat and felt and once inside saw Bridget's eyes on her. She said, "Morning all. I need a shower."

As she'd gone through the great room, she'd noticed that Jane was calm, sitting complacently with a mug of coffee on one of the room's sofas. *She didn't know.*

Evelyn slowly climbed the stairs she'd so enthusiastically and fatefully raced up as she removed her top not twenty-four hours before, in what seemed like a different lifetime ago. She went directly to the bathroom and stripped of her things, methodically, letting each damp piece drop randomly on the tiled floor as the water quickly warmed. She stood beneath the rain forest nozzle without moving, hoping, praying, that it could wash off some of the stain she knew would forever brand her, fighting tears with every intense droplet that struck and stung her.

Her stay in the shower was a long one until she could put it off no more.

She toweled off, collected her discarded pieces, and went to her room. She put the bundle of soiled things in a hamper. She then dressed and put the strap of her everyday bag over her shoulder. She took a look around the room and went down the hall. She glanced towards the master and shook her head at what a fool she had been.

She turned and then step by step she went down the now accursed staircase. At the bottom, she saw everyone had congregated on the deck, which is where she headed. Fran and Jane were on the right side of the group, sitting

173

in lounge chairs, each of their mugs on the small round table that separated them.

Todd wasn't there. And Bridget was off to the other side from Jane, her eyes fixed on Evelyn as she approached Fran's mother.

The sky had turned overcast, which felt appropriate.

When she reached the two Reynolds women, she bent down to Jane. "May I have a word?"

Jane looked at her daughter, who gave her an I-have-no-idea shrug, and then back at Evelyn. She was suddenly unnerved. *What could this near stranger have to say to me privately?*

Jane slowly rose and followed Evelyn through the house and out to the driveway.

"Yes?" Jane asked.

There was no other way to put it. "I had sex with Todd." That was it. Jane stared at the other woman as if she hoped she was a mere figment that would disappear. *Poof!* She stared.

"I'm sorry" was all Jane could say in response.

"Yesterday I drove out with him and one thing led to another and...we slept together."

For a moment, the world stopped for both women. Jane thought she'd want to know who started it, but she realized it didn't matter.

This woman had slept with her boyfriend. The boyfriend she hoped to marry. The boyfriend with whom she'd spoken about marriage. The boyfriend who wasn't Frank Reynolds, the bastard who left her and her three-year-old child decades before. When she was barely older than Eve was now.

This woman had slept with Todd when she knew who Todd was to Jane.

"I'm sorry," Jane repeated. But it didn't matter.

Evelyn had her car fob in her bag, which had been draped over her shoulder throughout. She said, "I'm so sorry" as she passed the stunned Jane. She unlocked her maroon BMW, got in, drove away, and was gone. A glance in her rearview mirror and it was the last she'd ever see of the East Hampton mansion of Peter and Amy Edgar.

For her part, Fran had gone to the house's foyer to see what was happening in the driveway. The others as a matter of discretion had stayed on the deck wondering what was going on there after both Peter and Amy had given Bridget a suspicious look. Bridget ignored it, instead turning to look out over the grand expanse of the Atlantic.

At the door, when Fran saw Evelyn get in the car and leave and her mother standing looking plainly desolate, she ran out. Jane was in tears, inconsolable by the time her daughter got to her. Fran led her mother into the house.

The others could hear the crying all the way out on the deck. Something significant and very, very bad had just taken place. Peter, Amy, and Bridget stood in a cluster, not daring to interrupt what was going on with Jane.

What that was was Fran leading her mother upstairs. In the bedroom, Jane said she just wanted to be alone as she lay down on the bed. Fran sat in a chair and watched as her mother's tears led to a disturbed sleep.

After they had gone up, Bridget directed Peter and Amy to a pair of chairs on the deck. She sat opposite them. She had their attention. She didn't mince words.

"Evelyn slept with Todd yesterday afternoon. I stumbled upon them doing it. Or at least I heard them doing it. I left them and she went back to the city. Todd did whatever Todd did.

"She begged to meet with me, and when we did—"

175

Amy interrupted. "That's why you disappeared last night?"

"Yeah, and we arranged to come back to the house together.

"By then, she had confessed what happened. She takes full responsibility for it. She said, and I believe her, that she had never done anything like that before and that it was the worst thing she has ever done. It's why we both went out alone this morning. I told her she had to confess to Jane, and that's what she just did and why she's...gone."

Bridget then excused herself, leaving the stunned couple to their thoughts. She went down that long, wooden staircase to the beach, thankful that she didn't see Todd anywhere.

For her part, Evelyn hadn't planned to run away. Then without a conscious thought, she was driving towards the city. She hadn't thought to prepare, but her key fob and apartment keys were in her bag and when she'd realized that, she just unlocked the BMW and was gone. Everything else, especially her phone and her wallet, were sitting in her room but she couldn't go back.

At least the traffic heading into the city was light, and her 5 Series was in its garage around the corner from her apartment about two hours after she left the house. It was a long walk to her building as she weaved through couples blissfully enjoying the Saturday. Finally, she opened her apartment door and dropped herself on her sofa and before she could decide what she was to do next, she fell asleep.

Evelyn was startled awake by her buzzer. "Who is it?" She had no idea how long she'd been out for or who it could possibly be.

She went to the panel by the wall and pushed the intercom button.

"Yes?" she asked, wearily.

"It's Bridget. Let me up."

WTF? Evelyn buzzed her in, opening her apartment door for this unexpected visitor. She stepped into the small hallway outside and waited. Completely unnerved by all of this, whatever *this* would turn out to be.

When Bridget arrived on her floor, Evelyn directed her inside and closed the door behind them. They exchanged nods but no words as they went inside.

Bridget had never seen Evelyn's place. It was a bit on the small side but tidy and well decorated, if perhaps too much was from IKEA.

"How'd you find me?" Evelyn asked. Bridget held up a small bag.

"Your driver's license. It was with some of the stuff you left behind. Especially your phone." Evelyn took the bag and went to get them both some water, the action helping to calm her.

When she returned, Bridget was on the sofa. Evelyn sat on the opposite end.

Neither said anything until Evelyn's "Thank you for bringing this to me. I didn't think to grab it before I...before I left. You could have FedExed it."

Bridget stayed quiet. Without a word, she got up and walked around the table. Her eyes locked on Evelyn's. She stepped across Evelyn's legs and straddled them. Their faces now seven or eight inches apart. Her right hand went to the other's left cheek and for the first time, the two shared a different, intimate touch. Evelyn sucked in her breath as the fingers slowly moved down. She grabbed Bridget's wrist and pulled her fingers to her lips and kissed them. It was the slightest of gestures but it forever sealed something deep within both women.

Bridget pulled her hand away and substituted her own lips on Evelyn's, very delicately as if anything more would shatter whatever it was that was tying them together.

After pulling her face back, Bridget put some strands of Evie's hair behind her left ear. She leaned in again and kissed the other woman on the lips but all the safeties were off and all delicacy and propriety were gone and they ground themselves into one another with Evelyn gripping Bridget's head.

Bridget was finally able to escape the physical hold that Evelyn had on her.

"I told you last night," she said as she looked straight into Evelyn's eyes and ran her own fingers down Evelyn's cheek, "that I love you for who you are. It's insane. It doesn't make sense. And I know you did something horrible that almost everyone will think unforgiveable. But I, at least, forgive you. It's up to other people to figure out what they're going to do. And I don't care about *other people* when it comes to you."

Evelyn gripped Bridget's hand against her cheek and pushed her head forward so she could meet Bridget's lips. Now they were fully engaged, their lips opening and their tongues taking turns invading the other's mouth.

Finally, Bridget awkwardly got her legs untangled with Evelyn's and stood. She extended a hand. Evelyn took it and got up. Bridget led her towards the bedroom. It was a mess. She didn't care. Neither did Evelyn.

When they were inside, Bridget closed the blinds and turned back.

Her last words, or at least words that were formed into sentences, were, "I'm not going to lie about what we're about to do. If they hate me for it, they hate me for it. I can't *not* do what we're about to do."

9.

BRIDGET AWOKE IN THE middle of their first night. She needed to pee. For the first time in her life, she was in bed with another person. She was initially startled by the arm draped over her and the light breathing behind her until she remembered. She remembered whose arm it was and whose breath it was and it washed over her like a flood of contentment she'd never imagined experiencing. One she never knew was possible.

Still. She had to pee.

She disentangled herself and made her way slowly in the dark, guided by her hands, to the bathroom. While there, she closed the door and turned on the light. After finishing, she looked at herself in the mirror. Her hair disheveled, she saw a woman she wouldn't have recognized two days earlier. Sleepy with eyes reddened by crying but displaying both satisfaction and hunger.

She turned off the light, waited a moment for her eyes to adjust to the dark, and slowly felt her way back to the bed. Evie had turned, now facing away from her, so Bridget wrapped her right arm around her and felt her sweat and glow. She lightly kissed her lover's neck, holding her lips to the skin for a long second and tasting it. And quickly drifted off.

Several hours later, Evelyn too had her startled moment. Since the demise of her engagement, she rarely, very rarely, woke up with another person and never in her own bed. When *she* remembered whose arm it was and whose breath it was, she shared her lover's contentment. The sun was up. She reached for her phone on the side table and touched its screen. 6:47.

She wallowed back into Bridget's embrace, fully awake. Her first thought was of what Bridget had done. Not having sex and then sleeping with her, significant as that surely was. No. She had deliberately sacrificed her connections with Peter and Amy and Petey. They would surely side with Fran not only in light of Evelyn's horrible behavior but because of Petey. Fran would make their life with the baby difficult if they sided with the SLUT who'd ruined her mother's life. She'd never again be allowed to stay if Fran didn't cut them off from Petey entirely.

Hearing the innocent ups and downs of Bridget's sleeping breath, Evelyn understood just how unworthy she was of her lover's sacrifice. Maybe, just maybe, someday Bridget would think her worth it. Now, though, she was afraid that Bridget would realize what she was giving up and would rush away, muttering *I'm-sorry-Evelyn-this-was-all-a-horrible-mistake.*

She was again letting emotions overwhelm her. She deserved to have Bridget leave, not stay.

When Evelyn had gone to the bathroom, she too had looked into the mirror. It wasn't the face she saw at the Hamptons house less than twenty-four hours earlier. It was a strange mix of happiness and fear, the fear that the happiness she just felt at the hands and tongue of a woman—*the woman*—she loved would be stripped from her, leaving her much worse off. That saying "it is better to have loved and lost than to never have loved at all" would be a cruel joke. And she'd deserved it and more.

She was still staring at her image when she heard light tapping on the door. She opened it, and Bridget, also naked, entered. She stood behind the taller woman and they both looked into the mirror. Where their eyes met.

"I told you I wouldn't leave you," Bridget whispered in Evelyn's ear with their eyes still locked in their reflections. "I meant it. I mean it. I will not leave you."

Evelyn nodded as a tear slipped down her right cheek.

"I was afraid you'd be dressed to leave when I got back to the bedroom. That's why I've been here for so long. I was afraid you'd—" and Bridget stopped her by turning her so they faced each other.

"Whatever happens, happens together."

That's all that needed to be said. They hugged and Bridget led Evie back to the bedroom by the hand.

The night before was rabid. Neither really knew what she was doing.

This morning was different. They were calm and each demanded to know what the other wanted. Surprisingly, given how inexperienced she was, Bridget took the lead. She told Evelyn to lay back and close her eyes. Bridget kissed the pair of eyelids, which elicited the first moan of the morning.

She sat back. Evie was beautiful. Her proportions perfect. She traced her right index finger from Evie's forehead down her nose and across her lips—receiving a slight peck as it passed—and down, down, down. Her head didn't move. Her head didn't move. Evelyn grabbed it and found herself getting lost in the blueness of Bridget's eyes.

"You are so beautiful," Bridget said. They both knew Bridget wasn't speaking only of Evie's body. *Bridget* suddenly moved and fell down on her back. She looked over at Evelyn. "Please take me."

Both women acted on pure, unadulterated instinct. It couldn't last. Within eight or ten minutes of their mutual ministrations, each felt the onset of a wonderful orgasm. Evie started, which set Bridget off.

When they each caught their breaths, Evie moved to reposition herself so she could lie face-to-face with Bridget and said in the clear light of day and in a post-coital flurry, "I love you Bridget, more than I could have imagined loving anyone."

Then again she wept. Bridget pulled her closer. And shortly sleep collected them both.

10.

WHEN BRIDGET RUSHED from the East Hampton house about an hour after Evelyn had fled with Fran and Jane to the latter's room and Todd was who knew where, she carried Evelyn's things and told Peter and Amy as she hurried to the front door that she couldn't *and wouldn't* leave Evelyn alone no matter what she'd done.

And Fran was sitting in a chair in Jane's room watching over her mother as she slept. When Jane awoke, she did so with a start. Her daughter reached for her hand and said it'd be alright and just that presence and touch and those words were calming to them both.

They went down and ran the well-meaning gauntlet of Peter and Amy asking how Jane was *handling things*. Fran waddled her hand to them before she and Jane continued to the deck and down the thirty steps to the beach and began a long, slow walk as mother and daughter, glad that they hadn't and didn't see Todd. By then, he'd slithered off to town.

Jane had always been the strong one in the Reynolds family. With some help from her relations, she shouldered the burden of raising a girl after being abandoned by her coward of a husband. Now the shock of what Todd had done to her sent her back to the day she came home and found her ex-husband Frank's scrawled note on the back of an envelope saying he wasn't coming back.

At least that episode was finally behind her. She had gotten a formal divorce after Fran's own investigation tracked him down to Arizona and was remarried with two kids. He didn't pay a dime for child support, but his being gone was worth it.

It was fortunate that Fran was herself recovering. She poured every ounce of herself into Eve. It is what got her through the horrible period of the past seven or eight months, including the banality of her hookup sex. Which might, just might, be behind her now that things were beginning to at least stabilize with Barry after several heart-to-heart walks and dinners and meetings.

Fran was very proud of her little daughter. Rambunctious and troublesome. But hers.

Peter was an active but could be no more than a part-time father and they were well past the time when anyone could question Fran's primacy. And everyone knew that she never again came close to what happened when she crashed her red Mercedes coupe into a post up in suburban White Plains.

Still, Fran did not want to be isolated again. She had worried that with the arrival of Petey, Peter and Amy would lose interest in Eve. They didn't. They tried not to show favorites. For the most part, Amy couldn't be blamed for doting on her own son, but she was always trying to do it conscious of Eve's presence. Amy had been a total bitch to Fran when they first met but now the reality had washed away the pretense and the two had fallen to liking one another in their own ways.

For Amy and Peter, Petey made them feel complete as a couple.

And Bridget had been integral to them all. *Why had she run after Evelyn?* Peter and Amy didn't know.

Nor did her old friend Fran. As she and her mother walked on the beach that Saturday, Jane defended Todd. "He's a man. He did what men do. She's pretty. She threw herself at him. I'll talk to him when we get back and we'll straighten it out."

Fran felt for her mother. She liked Todd well enough. He was good to Jane. Sweet. Attentive. He and Jane had chemistry and he helped her self-confidence and got her out of her shell. Granted, he had a bit of a wandering eye. He had slipped with Evelyn. She suspected he had *slipped* with other women, younger women, but he was a good man for her mother in the end.

As the two Reynoldses walked in the sand, they became more confident about one thing: Evelyn seduced Todd and *he* couldn't be blamed for doing something that any man would do.

When they climbed the steps to the house, they found Todd sitting with a beer off to the side. They went straight to him. He stood as they approached and he thought one or the other of the women would slap him.

They didn't. Instead, Jane stepped close to him and ran fingers down his cheek. He wrapped his arms around her while Fran watched carefully.

Without preamble, he admitted his *mistake*. While he didn't lie, he said that he couldn't be blamed for wanting to sleep with someone *as beautiful as Evelyn*. He knew that wasn't true. He had cheated on Jane but couldn't admit it. As he hadn't admitted to the prior times he'd failed to resist temptation.

In truth, he did care for Jane and he convinced himself that these had been nothing more than the scratching of an itch that was natural for a man like him to have. Meaningless.

Jane didn't blame him. Nor did Fran.

11.

BRIDGET WAS RIGHT. They did hate her for it. Well, not "they." Jane. Which is all that mattered. It was made clear to Peter that he had to choose. He really had no choice. He chose his daughter Eve and all that meant.

Bridget's position at the Foundation became untenable, especially with Fran working there. She was very good at it, but she had to go. Peter, without Fran's knowledge, got her a position at a non-profit that did the actual research; the Peter and Amy Edgar Foundation merely directed money to non-profits like it.

The things Bridget had at the East Hampton house were sent to her. She was allowed to collect her belongings at the Park Avenue apartment but, at her insistence, she was accompanied by a very uncomfortable staff member when she did. The apartment was otherwise empty of people.

Bridget was right too in that at the heart of it, it didn't matter as much to her as she might have thought it would. She regretted losing her friends a great deal, and she understood why they did what they did. But in her mind, she had no choice either. She would not leave the woman she loved. *Bridget* forgave Evelyn even if no one else had or ever would.

In the end, Bridget's forgiveness was all that mattered to Evelyn. She was far from the crying woman on the beach awed by the magnitude of the house to which Bridget brought her. It was just a house. Very big and with a great ocean view. But just another house.

Within a month after they first made love in Evelyn's small apartment, Bridget had gradually moved in. She kept her place in Woodlawn for a few months just in case but surrendered it three months later. She and Evelyn walked to work together whenever they could and as often as not met on the front steps of St. Patrick's, just north of Saks, for the walk home, much as she had with Amy in what was a far different time. And while space was a bit tight, the bed was big enough, if barely so, for them. Which was pretty much all that mattered.

Amy called Bridget now and then at first to touch base but it was never more than that. They were too afraid to have it be more. The break was too hard and the calls mercifully faded to never.

Evelyn's managers at Chase recognized her improvements and Dorothy, her immediate supervisor, suggested that she apply for an open position in the bank's risk-assessment department. The work there involved reviewing a borrower's or potential borrower's assets and assessing the strengths and weaknesses of its business. At the heart of the assessment was a judgment about the applicant's prospects. Evelyn interviewed and based upon her own department's recommendations— Dorothy made clear that she was *not* trying to dump Evelyn on another department but felt she could *blossom* in a new environment—she got the promotion.

More fundamentally, the couple was readily accepted by Bridget's folks up in the Bronx. All the Caseys wanted for their daughter was that she fall in love with someone, and it was clear that Evelyn was just such a *someone*.

The Irish diaspora in Woodlawn was far different from what it had been decades before and when the two girlfriends drove or took the 4 Train up on Sundays to see the Caseys, they were just another happy young, if gay, couple in the neighborhood visiting their folks and becoming regulars at one of the Irish pubs sprinkled throughout the neighborhood.

Things were a bit dicier with Evelyn's family. She grew up in an upper-middle-class home in Chappaqua, north of the city. Her parents, Dennis and Irene Manners, were lawyers working in midtown Manhattan, corporate partners in two different firms. She had one older brother, Jess, who moved to San Francisco after he graduated from Penn. He did something in tech, the non-descriptive word akin to a New Yorker's working *in finance.*

Still, they were disappointed, Evelyn's parents. They always thought their daughter would finally settle down, meet a doctor or lawyer or banker, have some kids, and settled into suburban bliss with regular visits on weekends. But in time they'd come to understand that the busted engagement was perhaps the best thing that had ever happened to her. That by-the-numbers marriage would have been drifting—again—into doing something simply because she was expected to do it.

To the contrary, Evelyn told them that she was infinitely more enthusiastic about some new person she'd met at her rich friends' house in the Hamptons but was cagey about the details.

The reality of the *sex* of that person couldn't be concealed forever, especially since they were more-than-roommates. So, she decided to cut straight to the chase with them and to do it in person. Bridget insisted she accompany her and with that, they would drive up to Chappaqua. Which they did on a Sunday morning several weeks after the two began living together.

As the BMW pulled into the driveway, the nerves kicked in for both. One of those ***Big Moments In My Life***. Evelyn didn't know how her parents would react to the *reality* of her being in love with another woman.

"Evie." Bridget said this with her hand on Evelyn's, which was on the gear-shifter. She looked at her lover, but Evie was looking straight ahead.

"Your parents love you, right?" Bridget said.

Evie nodded.

"If you tell them that I make you happier than you've ever been—nod if that's true," and Evie nodded and couldn't help but smile—"they'll be happy for us."

Evie looked to her lover, and they shared a chaste kiss.

"And if that doesn't work, tell them I'm pregnant."

"You are such a bitch," Evelyn laughed.

"Yeah, but I'm *your* bitch."

With that, the two got out of the car and, holding hands, walked to the door.

This wasn't unnoticed by Dennis and Irene. They were discreetly watching from the dining room. Evelyn hadn't said anything when she told them she was coming. He didn't mean to, but when he saw Bridget, Dennis whispered, *fuck*. With her husband frozen in place, Irene rushed to open the door before Evelyn knocked and reached to hug her daughter, moving her eyes to Bridget while she did.

Bridget was slightly behind Evelyn. Irene was a bit embarrassed. She'd always assumed, based upon her daughter's dating history—and engagement—that Evelyn was straight. The sight of the plain intimacy between the two girls destroyed that assumption in a flash and it didn't matter to Irene, who quickly became thrilled to meet someone who was so plainly right for her daughter. She looked toward the attractive blonde behind that daughter and said, "And you must be—" and she realized that she didn't know her name.

Evelyn jumped in. She had rehearsed this and gone over it with Bridget.

189

"Mom. This is Bridget Casey. She's my roommate. And girlfriend."

Irene rushed to hug Bridget and did it with genuine affection. It was enough that Bridget had her daughter's endorsement and she held her hug far longer than anyone expected and whispered so only Bridget could hear, "I'm so happy to meet you." Then, stepping back, she shooed the two into the house.

By then, Dennis Manners had recovered. His immediate reaction to seeing his daughter holding the hand of another woman was just that, a reaction. It was more in surprise than anything else. So, he hoped. He feared that his visceral reaction was a distaste—that's the word—for his daughter being with a woman. It was a reaction so contrary to his own professed statements. He had the uncomfortable taste of hypocrisy in his mouth.

He too gave Bridget a hug when they were introduced. The four headed into the living room with Irene asking if she could get the two anything. They asked for water, and Evelyn said she and Bridget would get it.

As Evelyn took a pair of glasses down and handed them to Bridget in the kitchen, she said quietly that she thought the initial meeting had gone well.

"I'm not really surprised," she said. Bridget gave her a kiss, and said, "I'm glad."

They got water from the tap and ice from the SubZero freezer and brought the glasses to the living room, where they sat side-by-side on the sofa, close to one another. Evelyn's parents sat opposite them, across a coffee table.

Evelyn took a long breath. Looking from one parent to the other, she said, "Mom. Dad."

She'd rehearsed this speech countless times as well, often with Bridget as her audience.

"I know how you always had certain expectations for me, and I know I've not met them very often. I've had certain expectations for me myself, and I've not met them either."

She continued, with Bridget tightening her grip and then holding her hand, lightly moving her fingers for support, to tell their story.

The beach.

The house.

The *reveal* that they loved each other. She paused at that, to give them time to take it in.

"I can't imagine how I got as far as I did without her. Now I don't want to be without her ever again. And I want you to be with us. So that's why I'm here... Bridget's the one who fixed all the ways you screwed me up."

With that note ending her piece, she sat back. Her mom got up and walked around the table. She gestured for Bridget to get up, and the two younger women did. She then gave another hug and said, this time for all to hear, "I'm not saying we screwed her up at all, but if you can shut her up about it, you're welcome at this house anytime."

And her father, still anxious about what he had said to himself, gave her another hug and offered to take them all to lunch.

Lunch in town itself went very well. All four felt comfortable, keeping mostly to safe topics. But the two younger ones engaged in behavior that was subtle but intentionally meant to display that they were *more than friends*. Word of course ricocheted around Chappaqua and by Sunday night a good part of town learned that Evelyn Manners might be a lesbian. Too many, but a small minority, of those with whom Evelyn grew up and went to school suddenly viewed her in a different, negative light. Blamed it on living in the city.

When word got to her ex-fiancé at his place in Williamsburg, Brooklyn, he told his buddies that he "dodged a bullet with that skank."

12.

EVELYN LOVED HER BURGUNDY BMW. Which was a good thing given how expensive it was to keep and garage. It was worth it and suddenly became so in a most unexpected way now that she had Bridget. It was her way of getting out of the city with her lover, to explore all there was to be explored. Never to the east, to the Hamptons. But north. The East River Drive to the interstate that opened so much to them.

They were free to act like old sailors, picking out a figurative North Star and letting it guide them. It took barely an hour to drive to Sleepy Hollow along the Hudson and enjoy the broad carriage trails on which J.D. Rockefeller and his guests would ride horses and carriages at his grand estate and where Evelyn could go for a run along the well-tended trails while Bridget went more slowly as a pedestrian.

Sometimes to the little unpretentious towns and villages, in Westchester and southwest Connecticut, stopping at estate sales in huge Greenwich houses that rivalled Peter's place in East Hampton. They'd drop into diners with their Hungryman Breakfasts that could feed them for a week. Or sometimes they'd wander in and out of boutiques that lined the streets in an affluent town and then sit by the window or in a little outside seating area in a farm-to-table eatery with fancy and expensive French toast or Eggs Benedict variations and divine cappuccino.

More than anything, her BMW took them to Bridget's folks in the northern Bronx or to her own parents in tony Chappaqua for the first meeting of the four parents. It was at the Manners's country club where they both played doubles tennis nearly every weekend.

By then, whatever tongues were going to wag had wagged themselves out. While Bridget's folks were a little more rough-around-the-edges than were Evelyn's, no one among the group cared and they laughed when Bridget's dad said his mother always wanted him to be a lawyer and Evelyn's said he always wanted to be a cop. "And shortstop for the Yankees."

At the club, while taking a break in the otherwise vacant ladies' room before their entrees were served, Bridget and Evelyn shared a joint sigh of relief about their parents from two so different worlds not only getting along but seemed genuinely happy and comfortable with one another.

"Do you think they're talking about how disappointed they are?" Bridget asked as they stood at the sinks washing their hands and looking at themselves in the mirror.

"About…you know, *us* and we both being, you know, women?"

Bridget laughed. "Not that. I think they are genuinely happy for us. I mean the *G* word."

Evelyn didn't understand at first, then it hit her.

"On that," she said, her eyes locking on Bridget's, "do you want kids?" *Ah, yes, Grandparents.* She paused. They'd never actually addressed this aspect of where they were going with their lives, especially with what both hoped was their joint lives. "Because if that's what you really want, I love you too much to stand in the way."

Both their expressions hardened, and Evelyn's showed a shimmer of fear about what Bridget would next say to her. It was something Evelyn had seen only once, that night standing on the sidewalk on Main Street in East Hampton when Evelyn had confessed to the horrible, horrible thing she'd done with Todd and to Jane. She recognized it as her lover's desperate fear that she would lose Bridget.

She needn't have worried. Bridget turned from the countertop and Evelyn did the same so they faced each other. She put her hands on Evelyn's waist but stayed apart from her. Things between them had moved so quickly. *But was talking about this crossing a line to permanent commitment?*

"I will tell you this," Bridget said. "Yes, I've always wanted kids. But suddenly I cannot imagine having a little girl or a little boy and not having you as their other, equal mother. This is not the Dark Ages, Sweetie. We'll figure it out. Together." She paused. "Understood?"

Evelyn nodded. They stepped closer for a tight hug and both had to step back again so they could wipe the tears that had begun to slide down their cheeks.

Before they'd fully regained control, however, the bathroom door opened and their heads turned towards the interruption.

It was Astrid, Bridget's mother.

"Are you girls alright here? You've been gone for a while and we were beginning to worry."

The girls looked at one another, and then Bridget turned back to her mother, sniffling a final tear. "We're fine, mom. More than fine. Just talking about some girlfriend things."

Astrid looked from one to the other.

"Alright then. Your dinners are getting cold," and she left. Bridget and Evelyn each slightly blushed and each wondering what their parents thought they'd really been doing for so long in the club's ladies' room.

Bridget slid her hand across the speckled marble countertop and placed it on Evelyn's. They turned to get back to their table just as Mrs. Elsbeth, a woman Evelyn had known since grammar school, was walking in and the two passed with nods directed at one another and Mrs. Elsbeth giving Bridget a not-so-subtle up and down examination.

13.

BRIDGET AND EVELYN WERE more than ready to get away in the new year. They spent Christmas Eve at the Caseys' in the Bronx and drove up to Chappaqua for Christmas itself. Not only were the Caseys there, but Evelyn's brother Jess flew in on December 23 and would be spending the rest of the year in New York before heading back to work in San Francisco.

Jeff was over six feet tall and objectively very handsome. Evelyn had warned Bridget that she was glad she got to her first because otherwise she would have surely fallen madly in love with her brother.

And when Bridget met him, she thought Evelyn might have been right.

Jess had far more self-confidence than did his sister and even she acknowledged that he had been more ambitious since they were kids, which reflected his honors degree from Penn and his success at his firm in the Bay Area. He got along instantly with all three Caseys.

Unfortunately for him, Evelyn's having plainly found her own future companion meant he was suddenly subjected to his family's curiosity about when *he'd* get around to finding his Mrs.—or Mr.—right. When Evelyn had come out to him in a phone call made only a few days after she'd come out to herself, he was genuinely thrilled for it, saying he never thought a man, especially the one to whom she was engaged, really worked for him.

"As to me," he told her in that first conversation, "I'm completely straight but I'll get myself a rainbow tattoo for you if you want."

She rejected that offer with a laugh but it brought her to tears. When things happened with Bridget, she was sure that Jess would be 100% supportive, but one never really knows beforehand. And over the initial weeks with Bridget, she was often calling Jess near midnight New York time for the support of her brother.

So, she was excited about a meeting between these two most important people in her life.

It wasn't too cold on Christmas and after they all attended mass as a matter of tradition and not religion and were settled back at the house, Bridget asked Evelyn if she'd be okay with her going for a solo walk with Jess. No more than half an hour and then Evelyn could join them.

"He's very important to you," she said, "and I'd like to get to know him a bit and to have him get to know me a bit."

Ultimately, because Evelyn and her brother were so alike in fundamental ways, Jess in just that simple walk through the quiet streets of the affluent New York suburb had no difficulty in considering Bridget almost like a second sister and she felt she'd found a brother.

So, the three left their older generation to have their drinks and watch their basketball and gossip lovingly about their children until it was beginning to get dark and it was time for the final preparation of the holiday feast.

14.

FOR THEIR VACATION as a couple, in the next February, Bridget and Evelyn headed a bit farther north, to Great Barrington, Massachusetts. Just over the border from New York. On Airbnb, they found a small place with a kitchen and booked it for a week, arriving late on the Sunday afternoon.

It was cold and icy in spots, but the forecast didn't have snow for the week. The place was a converted garage in a wooded area. Well away from the main house. A flight of stairs and a large room with a large (and inviting) bed and large windows looking out to the woods as well as a small kitchen and bathroom and a more casual space on the ground floor. There was a small deck to the rear but it was far too early in the year to be used, and bits of snow and ice had accumulated around the bottoms of its posts.

They didn't know the area and headed into town to explore. The couple scoped out possible restaurants for dinner. That done, they headed back to the house and they could not overcome temptation and had quickly pulled the comforter from that large bed and their clothes from their bodies and made the sort of spontaneous fevered love that only people with a deep connection can pull off.

Once done and quickly getting chilled, Bridget pulled the comforter over their satisfied bodies and wrapped an arm around her lover and they soon, very soon, drifted off to the sleep of the angels.

It was dark when they awoke. Evelyn reached for her phone.

"It's almost seven," she told Bridget with some alarm.

"Stay," was the sleepy response but after Evelyn said they'd better get up or the local police would find their cold bodies, they reluctantly got out of bed, got dressed, and headed into town for their first dinner as a vacationing couple.

With one craving taken care of, they each had a burger and fries and wine at a place on the town's Main Street (or at least half of the burgers, the rest of them and a pile of fries coming back to the B&B with them). All topped off with decaf cappuccinos.

From that auspicious first day, they fell into a routine. The area was quieter than normal because many of the New Yorkers who came up for the weekends were back in their well-insulated apartments.

Beginning on Monday, they just vacationed. Each had sworn to the other that they would check their email only thrice a day: Before they went out, at lunchtime, and before they went out for dinner. And they kept to it for the most part; Bridget snuck phone calls to her office twice while Evelyn had run into a store for something.

After sampling the restaurants in town and in nearby Stockbridge and especially Lenox, Bridget insisted on going to a particular one next to the Performing Arts Center in Great Barrington on Friday. They sat across from each other at a booth close to the bar near where a fire was roaring. Each had a salad and quiche and agreed to share dessert—tiramisu. When that arrived, Bridget grabbed Evelyn's hands before she could get her fork.

"I've loved this week with you."

"So have I." Evelyn's gears were turning. *Why isn't Bridget letting me get my fork?*

She knew the answer before the question was asked.

"Will you—?"

"Of course, I will."

Bridget paused with a slight, feigned pout. "You didn't let me finish."

Evelyn smiled. "I promise. From now on I promise I'll always let you *finish*" and she gave her best shit-eating grin after she extended that last word.

"You are such a bitch."

"Yeah, but I'm *your* bitch."

"Touché."

Evelyn looked concerned. "Is that it?"

"You're so smart, you tell me."

Evelyn draped her left hand above the table. Palm down. She wiggled her ring finger as she stared at the woman of her dreams.

"If you insist."

Bridget reached into her pocket and passed the ring over the knuckle and after exchanged *I love you*s, Evelyn heard applause. Behind her were four smiling parents and the respective mothers rushed to congratulate their respective daughters and the respective fathers did the same.

Bridget's dad, Danny, said, "We thought you'd never get there." He lifted a Guinness—he was, after all, an Irish cop in New York—and everyone in the room and behind the bar applauded, and Evelyn wanted to slink below the table but her fiancée wouldn't let her.

When they were finally rid of their parents, who had been at a big table in the dining room for the duration and were staying in a nearby B&B, they got back to their place. They were exhausted. Yet somehow very horny. They took turns in the bathroom to get ready to christen the launching of this new, frightening, and perhaps inevitable stage of their joint lives.

In the cold of the room, each put on a white terry cloth robe as they left the bathroom, Evelyn first. She waited on the edge of the turned-down bed and watched mesmerized as Bridget undid the belt to her robe and let it drop off her shoulders to the floor and shamelessly displayed the perfection that her fiancée had long ago recognized.

She stepped to her lover.

One.

Two.

Three.

They both satisfied the primal hunger and desire that seemed to increase with each time they made love until on that memorable night each was exhausted and inevitably each had fallen into a sated, most happy dreamland.

About two weeks later, Evelyn gave Bridget her ring, picked out together in the city's midtown diamond district. It was, as was Evelyn's, a small stone in a simple setting. Both rings, as Goldilocks would say, were not-too-big/not-too-small. And, as was so much the case in the lives of these two women, *perfect*.

15.

THINGS RETURNED PRETTY MUCH to normal for the newly-minted fiancées, Evelyn at Chase and Bridget at her non-profit not too many blocks away.

Less than a month later, Bridget was bringing her lunch back to her office in the labyrinth that is Rockefeller Center. As she often did, she passed the F.A.O. Schwarz store in one of the center's Art Deco buildings and, as it often did, it made her think of Petey. He'd be turning one soon, and the toy store reminded her of how terribly she missed him. Carrying the bag that held the salad she would eat at her desk, she took a detour, going in yet again to imagine the birthday gift for the precious child she'd never see again, a gift she would never send.

As she turned down one of the aisles, she saw Amy studying something she'd lifted from a shelf. Bridget quickly turned and fled the store, before Amy could spot her. They hadn't seen each other in some seven months, and she missed her terribly.

She was not the love of her life. That was Evelyn. But Amy had occupied a different but still very important role after all their walks together and that role now stood empty for Bridget. She had been a best friend and no one came close to being a substitute for her. She was left with Evelyn and some old acquaintances from her time at Lenox Hill.

It was a fine day, but Bridget no longer noticed or cared. She was about thirty steps away from the store when she felt a hand touch her right arm. She stopped. She wasn't prepared for this. She wouldn't turn.

Amy circled in front of her. Neither said a word. They stood there, in the middle of the sidewalk on 49th Street.

Bridget couldn't say anything. She struggled to maintain her dignity and composure.

Amy filled the silence. "I have missed you so much."

They stepped to the side to let people pass. "I've missed you, too." Amy, noticing the ring offered congratulations, a bit hesitant until Bridget said, "Evelyn."

Amy knew little about what had happened between the other two since that horrible Saturday when Bridget left to bring Evelyn her things. She knew Bridget was gone from the Foundation—she and Peter said it was necessary to keep Fran happy—and gone to work for her current non-profit. Bridget and Evelyn, though, had otherwise disappeared, with no social media presence. While they had spoken, at least at first, Bridget was closed-mouthed in those conversations about what was going on with Evelyn. Obviously, it was a lot.

They began to walk. They saw an open spot on the benches along the promenade that connected the famous rink (the tree was gone) and Fifth Avenue itself. They sat. Bridget said she had to get back, but Amy pleaded with her to stay.

Bridget looked at Amy.

"I can't go down this road with you. I just can't. I made my decision and while I've regretted losing you and Peter and Petey, I don't regret going with Evelyn and I never will."

She stood.

Amy looked up at her. "Do you have the same number? I need to think and speak to Peter. Then I'll call you." She rose too. "You can't imagine how much I've missed you." With a sharp hug and a final, "Please?" Bridget nodded. It had to be enough for Amy, who turned and walked up the promenade towards Fifth Avenue and the imposing façade of Saks across it.

Bridget watched and saw her shoulders shake. Amy was crying. She didn't look back.

16.

WHEN BRIDGET CAME THROUGH the door that night, hung up her coat on a hook in their small foyer, and kissed Evelyn, her fiancée immediately knew the kiss was…off. Bridget said she was tired and plopped down on the sofa. There was something but Bridget would explain when she was ready to explain. Evie went to the kitchen to throw the dinner she picked up in the microwave.

"Wine?" she asked.

"Please."

Evelyn poured a glass and took it and her own to the living room. She sat next to her lover and handed her the glass and waited. After Bridget took a sip, she turned.

"I saw Amy."

The two hadn't spoken about her, or the others, for a while. It had become *verboten*, like a third rail that would electrocute on touch. Each knew, though, that one or the other might run into her or one of the others in the city. It's perhaps a paradox about Manhattan. But because people travel on sidewalks or on the subway to get anywhere, they're always running into people they know.

"I was in F.A.O. Schwarz thinking of Petey and the gift I wouldn't get him when I saw her," Bridget said as she looked at the burgundy she was swirling in her glass. "I got out of there as fast as I could and thought I'd gotten away, that she hadn't seen me, but she caught me on the sidewalk."

The two sat looking in front of themselves. Evie had been dreading this. *Would seeing Amy remind Bridget of how much she'd given up when she opted for her?* She still was insecure about this one, all-important part of her life.

Bridget placed her glass on the coffee table and took Evie's and put it beside hers. Grabbing both of Evelyn's wrists, she forced her to look into her eyes. Both women's eyes were watering.

"Evelyn. My love. I have never second-guessed my decision to be with you. Being with you is who I am. I know that now and I have known it since I committed, fully committed myself to you. Of course, I miss Amy and I miss Peter and I miss Petey more than *almost* anything. But I would miss you more. Okay?"

Evelyn nodded.

"Say it." Bridget voice was hard. "Say you understand that I need you more than anything." She paused and pressed tighter on Evelyn's hands. "Say it."

"I understand...But why?"

"Listen. I'm sitting in this place with you when I could be sitting on a deck overlooking the Atlantic with a wine five times as expensive as this one." She nodded to her glass. "Yeah, I know it's March, but you know what I mean. Sitting on Park Avenue. But if I'm not sitting with you, none of that matters. None of it."

"But—"

"Evie, it just is. Okay? I don't have to know how a plane flies to Paris. I just know it does."

Evelyn found herself being led to the bedroom; the microwave's five beeps ignored. Bridget placed her hands on Evie's waist and positioned her next to and with her back to the bed. She leaned in and gave a kiss to the left side of Evie's neck. Leaning back again, her hands unbuttoned Evie's blouse. Her fiancée began to shake from the arousal building within her.

Bridget continued until she pulled the blouse from her lover's skirt and, finishing the unbuttoning, she pushed the blouse over Evie's shoulders and over her arms and folded it neatly. She walked away and placed it on the dresser.

Evie didn't move.

Bridget came back. She bent down and removed Evie's pumps, this time placing the shoes on the floor by the dresser.

Evie didn't move.

Bridget bent down and kissed Evie's navel. She felt the shivering of Evie's skin. Inhaled the sweetness of Evie's sweat. She reached behind Evie and undid the skirt's button and quickly removed it after Evie lifted one and then her other foot. It was placed atop the blouse.

Evie didn't move.

Bridget was never not surprised by what she saw. Soon she'd removed what remained of Evelyn's clothing, leaving her standing naked and nervous, her shaking visible from clear across the room.

There were times when their *fucking* had a glorious spontaneous aspect. This would not be one of them. Bridget quickly stripped as Evelyn stood like a statue watching and the bed, too, was quickly stripped of its comforter and blanket and the two descended into the world of passion that had come to define their intimacy.

And they always, always savored the time when it was quiet and that passion had coursed through the entireties of their bodies, with their own thoughts of contentment. Bridget turned slightly so she could run her fingers along Evelyn.

"You must never," she said in a low voice, "*ever* doubt how important you are to me."

Evelyn fought to keep some composure and didn't move as Bridget continued,

"Evelyn Manners. Were I asked to give up everything in the world to be like this with you and to be loved by you, I would do it in a heartbeat." She thought half the city could hear how loudly her heart pounded.

She waited. Evelyn, eyes fixed on the room's ceiling but her hand grasping for Bridget's, said, "I will die and still not know what I have done to deserve you, Bridget Casey."

She turned to face the other woman. Their lips met for only a moment before they both dropped down on their backs, with Bridget awkwardly getting the blanket that had been cast aside over them to battle the sudden chill they felt as the physical heat they had generated slid away from them.

Evelyn turned on her side so she could be spooned and Bridget promptly obliged.

Bridget's eyes were closed. She was thinking. Of nothing and of everything. She gave Evie a light kiss on the nape of her neck and pulled even closer.

"There is no place in the world I would rather be, or that I can dream of being, than right here with you."

A more basic hunger descended upon them.

"Let's eat," Bridget said. They got up, put on their robes, and reset the microwave.

17.

THINGS WERE MORE SEDATE but no less intense about the chance meeting earlier that day less than a mile to the southwest, in Peter and Amy's apartment. They sat on one of the couches in the living room. Amy's conversation with Peter started much as Bridget's had with Evelyn.

"I was at F.A.O. Schwarz," she began and then recited the story in what seemed to Peter like a single breath, "when my attention was caught by a woman quickly turning away. I saw enough to think it might be Bridget. I replaced the box I'd been looking at on its shelf and hurried to see whether I was right. I'd reached the cashiers when I—"

She abruptly stood and began pacing back and forth in front of the couch, her hands gesturing calmly. "— when I saw it was Bridget. She was hurrying through the revolving door and heading east on 49th Street. I ran out after her, cutting through the lunchtime crowd."

Amy stopped and dropped down into an armchair that sat across from the couch. "She was rushing away. She must have seen me in the store. There was no other explanation. By the time I reached her, I was out of breath. I tapped her upper arm, and she froze. Just stopped in the middle of the sidewalk and I stopped too and someone behind me almost hit me and called me an *asshole* as he went by."

She laughed at that. "Me. An asshole?"

"You?" Peter said, breaking his silence. "Never."

"Fuck you," his wife said with a sweetness of tone only a true couple can use with one another and got up again and recovered her seriousness as she resumed her seat beside him. She leaned against her husband. "I was out of breath. She wouldn't turn. She must have known who I was."

Amy continued. She told him she'd stepped in front of Bridget. Who she hadn't seen or spoken to in months. She pleaded with Bridget to at least speak to her so they stepped to the side to get out of harm's way and faced each other.

"I told her how much I'd missed her, and she said the same thing to me. We were on the verge of tears but then I saw the little diamond ring on her left ring finger. She noticed. Without my asking she said *Evelyn*."

Peter looked surprised.

Amy continued. "I was genuinely happy for her. We walked east and found space on the Promenade and sat."

Amy recited the conversation they'd had and ended by saying she told Bridget she had to speak to Peter but perhaps, maybe, they could at least try talking on the phone.

Bridget, she finished, promised to wait for Amy's call.

Peter said he missed Bridget, too. She had been his platonic best friend until things had blown up. But because things *had* blown up with what Todd and Evelyn did, he said he needed to speak with Fran about it.

Amy and Peter had sometimes spoken of it. Of what would happen if they ran into Bridget or Evelyn. And they'd kicked that can down the road. But no more. They knew they would forgive Evelyn after Bridget did so. The problem was always Fran. And her control over Eve.

"We both know," Amy said, "you have to speak with her. Maybe she'll come around."

"I doubt it," her husband said. "But you're right. I have to try."

She leaned against him on the couch. "You do have leverage," she said. "Money does have its non-financial usefulness."

She caught his slight, somewhat sinister smile. He leaned to her and kissed her.

"You are evil," he said. She pulled his lips to hers and let him pull back.

"Which is why you love me."

They were both familiar with the confrontation that Amy had had long before at Starbucks in which she had...*threatened* Fran with social-media suicide if she didn't accept Peter's very generous proposal about the future. And Fran had agreed to it and things had worked out for everyone. Everyone, that is, until what Evelyn had done with Todd and everything went to hell.

Peter stood. He lifted his phone from the coffee table and went to the apartment's sanctuary. Its dark library.

He called Fran. After their normal exchange about how Eve was, Peter brought up Bridget.

"Finally." Her tone altered markedly. "I was wondering how long you'd wait to mention her. Look, I have no problems with her. It's that slut who fucked Todd that matters. Bridget can come by whenever she wants. She's such a fucking saint all the time, but she's tolerable. But forget about that other one."

"But—"

"Peter, remember, *you* didn't abandon Bridget. She abandoned *you*. Why she went with that skanky bitch is beyond me. I never liked her. Are they even together?"

"They're engaged." Peter didn't intend for that bit of information to pop out and it was too late.

"Perfect. So, she fucks my mother's boyfriend and, what?, it turns her into a dyke. Fucking perfect."

"But your mother's not even with him anymore."

"Fuck you, Peter. She was with him then and that's all that matters. Fuck you."

And she hung up.

When Peter rejoined Amy in the living room, he said it went worse than they expected. And they weren't expecting much.

The pair sat quietly. Finally, Amy spoke. "I know you wanted to avoid it, but it's nuclear option time. I don't want to hurt your relationship with Eve, but I need to try to get back with Bridget. We can't let the whims of Fran dictate our lives forever. I won't embarrass her or Jane. I won't bring Bridget...and Evelyn to the house. I just want to be able to see her. She was my best friend. I miss that. You have no—"

Peter interrupted to say he knew what she felt. He missed Bridget's friendship too. It had predated Amy's.

"Peter, we both know Fran cares more for Eve than anything. We both know she can't afford to cut you off. And if she tries, you have your rights under the agreement. If she wants to play hardball, in the end, your guy controls Eve's money. Fran's not going to chance losing that. That, the money, was half the point of her baby trapping you."

Peter wasn't so sure. He agreed to speak with his attorney about it in the morning before they took any action. But the cat was out of the bag.

Peter had to sit down with Fran. He called her again and before she could hang up or hurl a string of obscenities at him, he got her to agree to meet at a neutral coffee shop a block-and-a-half from her Queens apartment. He drove the Porsche SUV across the Triborough and down to Astoria on the next Saturday morning.

He told Fran that it was Amy who sought Bridget out and not the other way around. That she'd chased Bridget on the sidewalk outside F.A.O. Schwarz.

Fran didn't need as much convincing as Peter expected. When she hung up on him the day Amy stopped Bridget, it hit her. Bridget had abandoned her too. And she *missed* her. She loved working with her at the Foundation, and everyone missed her there. She missed being able to gossip with her at the office or out in the Hamptons.

Personally, she didn't care that much one way or the other about Evelyn, but the fact that Bridget did was what mattered. And it would be nice to have Bridget get back with Eve. And, she admitted, with Petey as well.

Ultimately, Peter didn't have to play hardball. There were two reasons.

First, Fran feared the spigot for Eve's trust would be shut off if she tried to leave New York, the only way to get away, something Peter's lawyers made sure of.

Second, she surprised herself by acknowledging that she too missed Bridget. She always found her annoying, but she always found her...*there*. She wouldn't have made it through without her. She knew she was unkind in mocking her as *Saint Bridget*. What happened with Evelyn proved she was human and loyal, walking away from the access Peter and Amy gave her and never looking back.

She told Peter that as long as no one tried to force Evelyn on her, she could live with Bridget and she would make nice with her if she really had to see her. When she said this, Peter felt a huge load lifted. He called Amy when he was back in the SUV, telling her that this time it had gone far better than they both had expected. Fran, he told her, promised to speak to Jane.

Jane quickly came around. Todd had broken up with her about four months after he slept with Evelyn. That cheating and his admission that it wasn't the first time were signs of growing restlessness and one day he told her he wanted to see other women. And that's how it fizzled out.

Things would likely never return to the way they were, Fran told her mother, especially the family atmosphere that had prevailed in East Hampton. She said that Amy promised Jane she would never have to face Evelyn if she didn't want to. That Evelyn wouldn't be coming to the house.

A complication, though, arose almost immediately. Petey's first birthday was fast approaching. Under the rules of the truce, that meant *either* Bridget or Jane. Not both.

Fran was grasping at getting more of the normalcy back and making Petey's birthday more special for him. She sat her mother down.

"Evelyn did a horrible thing. She admits it."

"She's never admitted it to me."

"Because you won't let her," Fran pointed out. "She's admitted it to Bridget and apparently told Bridget the day it happened that it was her fault. You've always been excusing Todd. Todd wasn't just another man. In the end, he was an asshole who cheated on you. They're both responsible then. Except he's the one who never admitted it."

"She cheated on me, too."

"Mom, I get it. But now you're cutting off your nose to spite your face. I don't care about her. I do care about Bridget. And Petey and Eve. I need Bridget. I wouldn't be here yelling at you if it weren't for her. We both know that. She was the one I called when I needed someone. Now I have no one. Amy still holds something against me. Bridget's over that."

"What do you want from me?" Jane asked.

"Petey's birthday is coming up. I want to have them go to his party, Bridget and Evelyn both. I'm not saying you have to do anything beyond tolerate being in the same room as them for a one-year-old's birthday. That's all. And then they'll be gone."

With her daughter's speech, and her daughter's admission of how important Bridget was to her, Jane relented. *Just this once* she would go along. She made it clear that she *Was Not Happy* about it, but for one hour she could, as Fran asked, *tolerate it.*

The party was held at a large space on the Upper East Side dedicated to such events. Petey was one, but his mom insisted on lots of colors and lots of balloons and lots of noise.

Bridget and Evelyn were beyond nervous. Amy had only given Bridget the okay a couple of days before, optimistically promising that everything would be alright. The couple had to buck each other up as they took the elevator to the play space. They saw the party through a glass door.

"Ready?" Bridget said, gripping her fiancée's hand very tightly.

"As ready as we'll ever be."

They went in. Evelyn carried the toy that Bridget did get at that F.A.O. Schwarz.

Then something they hadn't expected occurred. It had been nearly seven months since little Eve had seen Bridget but the moment she saw her, the girl's expression changed from the not-so-subtle jealousy she felt for Petey getting all of the attention to excitement about seeing her Auntie. She hadn't been told Bridget was coming.

Eve raced to Bridget and grabbed her legs. They'd said that Bridget had to go away before she could say goodbye and that they didn't know whether she would be back. And now she was back. Fran rushed over to get her child, nearly running into Bridget. And Evelyn.

Bridget wasn't prepared for this. She thought she would be. She leaned over Eve, who was refusing to cede her spot holding Bridget's thighs, and hugged her. She didn't realize how much she actually missed Fran. After Fran gave her a perfunctory nod, Evelyn drifted away to give the two (or the three) time and space.

By then the commotion had caught the attention of the adults in the room. Peter and Amy kept a discreet distance away as well. Only Jane looked away. She'd been warned but didn't know how she'd react when she saw Evelyn for the first time since she'd driven off in her BMW after shattering Jane's world. When she saw her, Jane turned to stare out the window at the building across the avenue. She, too, hadn't prepared herself adequately.

Not long after, Jane saw Evelyn's approach reflected in the window. She took a deep breath and turned to face this inevitability. The two locked eyes.

"Whatever you think of me, I've thought worse," Evelyn began, in a line she'd rehearsed a thousand times. "What I did to you was unforgivable—"

"And yet here you are, seeking forgiveness." It was a cold observation from the woman Evelyn had cheated on, deservedly so.

"Yes. Here I'm seeking...asking for your forgiveness. It was the worst thing I've done in my life. That's all I can say."

With that, Evelyn turned and headed back to the now large group surrounding her fiancée.

18

ABOUT A WEEK BEFORE Bridget's thirtieth birthday and a month after Petey's party, Amy called her restored friend. It was the early days in the détente that everyone hoped was evolving to something more permanent. "Bridget," she asked, "can you and Evelyn join Peter and me for a quiet dinner at the apartment? Petey's nanny will be here." They had never dined alone as a foursome. Evelyn had never been to the apartment and Bridget hadn't been there since she removed her things months and months before.

The doorman in front didn't recognize Bridget as they entered the lobby through the revolving door, but the one at the reception desk immediately did. He ran around to greet her, as if she'd never been gone and hugged her. Evelyn stepped to the side.

"Ms. Casey. Welcome back. They said you'd gone away and they didn't know whether you'd make it back."

"Thank you, Carl." She broke into a wide smile at the recognition. "Yes, I'm back. I hope for good. I'm well. This is my fiancée, Evelyn."

Evelyn and Carl shook hands and exchanged greetings when Bridget asked, "How have you been?"

"You know. Same old, same old." A smile brightened his face. "It's really good to see you again. I'll let the Edgars know you're here."

After he did and they okayed it, he used his key in the elevator to send the two women to the ninth floor.

When the elevator door opened, the three Edgars were waiting. The first thing, of course, was for Bridget to hug Petey. And Evelyn followed suit. He quickly squirmed away and waddled to his mother, who held his hand as Peter had and then she gave hugs. The nanny was standing in the living room, and when Peter and Amy turned, she came to collect Petey and take him to his room.

Bridget was shocked when they stepped into the living room. The walls were empty. Freshly painted but not a thing was hanging. In the place of the haphazard paintings that were hung for size and color was...nothing.

"About that." Peter said. "I want to hire you for something."

"Peter. You know I'm happy where I am."

"This is more of a consultancy gig. I want you to curate our living room. Eight figures. Well, low eight-figures. If you can get *Madame X*, that'll do." He was referring to the priceless John Singer Sargent painting that had created a Parisian scandal in its original form and was now among the most precious of the paintings owned by and displayed at the Met Museum less than a half-mile away.

"Otherwise," he continued, "your job, should you decide to accept it"—and Amy piped in with "and we know you will"—"is to make this your playground. We trust you. What do you say?"

Bridget didn't know what to say. Evelyn squeezed her hand. This was a dream. Empty walls. A blank canvas. And a very, very big check. Heaven for an art *aficionado*. And for Astrid, her mother and tutor.

The others waited. No one moved.

"Of course, I'll do it. Oh my God. I can't thank you enough." She spun completely around to remind her of the space and stepped first to Peter and then to Amy and then back to Peter and then back to Evelyn, controlling her joyful tears as well as she could.

Peter added. "The best part is that it's your birthday present, but you have to do all the work. Being rich has its advantages."

Being friends with someone rich also has its advantages.

Once word got around, Bridget and Evelyn could have survived on the finger food and booze served at galleries uptown and down, eastside and west, Brooklyn, that they visited on their quest for the right pieces. She got her mother, Astrid, the source of her passion for art, to join as a co-conspirator, and the three, four when Amy joined, made the rounds. Christie's and Sotheby's too.

Even better for Bridget were the sudden invitations to events at museums. She was suddenly a *player.* Not only the Met and MoMA, but the Whitney and the Guggenheim. She was no dilettante. She and her mother knew their stuff. Being allowed to wander alone through museum galleries was a dream. More than one curator suggested she might like to become a doyen for their collections. But Bridget and her mother, with day jobs, declined.

Bit by bit, piece by piece, the mundane walls of what had been a staid living room were transformed into something actually alive. Bridget found modern pieces that complemented those from the nineteenth and early twentieth centuries. Her focus wasn't on obtaining pieces from well-known masters but on lesser-known works of artists well regarded as being equal to or at times surpassing the better known and more expensive. Several small modern sculptures were well-placed on podiums and several colorful and recent abstract oils mingled among the more traditional works.

When it was done, Bridget was the guest of honor at a dinner party at the apartment. Her folks and Evelyn's came joined by a mix of friends of Amy and Peter. Although Fran and Jane were invited, they declined. Bridget and Evelyn heard the story of Amy's Bryant Park now-famous freak-out in great detail from Amy's work-colleagues Sarah and Evan. Bridget also had the chance to explain her selections to several gallery owners who she asked be invited.

At the end of the night, after Bridget received a post-toast ovation, she and Evelyn walked home in a bit of a haze. In her metaphoric pocket, she carried Peter's promise that once she'd recovered from this bit of Manhattan magic, she could do the same for the wide open spaces in the house in East Hampton.

19

BRIDGET DIDN'T HAVE UNLIMITED time to do Peter and Amy's curating, much as she would have liked to. She (and Evelyn and Astrid) had a job. And there was a wedding to prepare for.

Evelyn took the laboring oar on that. They thought of having it at her parents' church in the Bronx but that thought was quickly extinguished when they realized a gay wedding was *verboten* at a Catholic church. And when they realized that the last place they wanted to get married was at an institution that not only frowned upon their relationship but to many of its members and clergy positively disdained it.

Rather than delve into alternative, more hospitable faiths, Bridget and Evelyn agreed to ask Peter and Amy if they could have the ceremony in the house in East Hampton. This was a problem. As part of the treaty negotiations, Amy had assured Jane that Evelyn would never again set foot in the house. It was Jane's sanctuary.

But Jane had, since Petey's birthday party, softened her view. She'd seen how Peter had forgiven her daughter and they'd all been the better for it. Maybe it was time to take this next, perhaps final step with the woman who'd betrayed her albeit just that one time as Fran had betrayed Peter.

On a Thursday in mid-May, Evelyn was at work at the bank and received a call from the lobby that a *Jane Reynolds* was there to see her. It took her a moment to understand. When she did, she said, "tell her I'll be right down." In the lobby, gazing out onto the building's plaza on Park Avenue, was Jane. She was dressed as Evelyn had never seen her, in the far more formal attire of a woman who worked at a large Manhattan law firm. She turned when Evelyn addressed her. They hadn't spoken since Evelyn stepped away at Petey's party.

They found two chairs in the lobby.

"You asked for my forgiveness," Jane began. "For a long time, I never thought I could give it to you. Even while waiting here for you, I wasn't sure. I am now, seeing you."

She reached for Evelyn's hand. "You've never tried to justify what you did, and I respect that. You were honest about it. To me and, as far as I can tell, to everyone. I love my daughter and I love my granddaughter. I may never love you, but if you give me a chance, I'll try to."

"I promise I will do my best to earn it," Evelyn said, truly surprised and touched by what Jane had said.

They stood and hugged.

"That's all I have to say. I have to go now."

The older woman stood. She turned.

"Fran said you asked about getting married at the house in East Hampton. It may not be much, but you have my blessing."

With that Jane walked to and through the revolving door out onto Park Avenue. Evelyn stood by one of the large windows facing the street and watched her pass north and gave her a slight wave as she did.

20

THEY LOVED THE SIMPLE things so Bridget and Evelyn decided on simplicity for their wedding. With Jane's blessing in hand, they had no reason to delay having the ceremony near the sandy stretch of beach where they'd met.

On a fittingly overcast Saturday morning in late June with rain threatening but not yet arrived, they awoke in separate rooms at the East Hampton house. That felt strange. They'd slept together every night since Bridget moved into Evelyn's cramped apartment on the Upper East Side. Not to tempt fate, they decided to abide by someone's idea of tradition and kept themselves separate the night before and each fell into the sweet dream that they would never sleep alone again.

Amy and Peter offered to have a pre-wedding event for them in the city, for friends and colleagues, but the two declined. Bridget attended a surprise get-together with a group of runners who were members of the running club that Evelyn had joined a few months earlier. That was in the low-ceilinged basement of an eastside restaurant. Then several of Evelyn's co-workers at Chase took them to a pub on East 47th Street for a celebratory lunch on the Thursday before the wedding.

Then Wedding Day dawned! Bright and clear.

By nine, everyone was up and starting to get ready. By ten, the deck was crowded with the hosts, Peter, Amy, and Petey; the proud mothers and Evelyn's brother, Jess; Jane and Fran and Barry; and the same local judge who'd fulfilled the role for Amy and Peter in this very house was acting as the officiant.

Little Eve slowly marched into the great room. She was very serious and took each step slowly and rhythmically. On her right arm was a straw basket with a white ribbon tied on its handle, and she was using her left hand to sprinkle her way with a combination of white and burgundy rose petals.

She was followed by Evelyn accompanied by her father, and they were followed by Bridget and her dad. Each of the brides wore simple but elegant white dresses, not quite matching but wonderfully complementary to each other. Each carried a bouquet of roses. Evelyn's were the white and Bridget's were the burgundy of the petals in Eve's basket, their scattering meant to reflect the combination of their two lives.

The brides' fathers wore dark suits with red ties and white or burgundy rose boutonnieres, in each case matching the color of their daughter's bouquet. Each presented his daughter to their mothers who would stand next to them for the ceremony.

No objections were made.

Vows and rings were exchanged.

Kisses were given.

Kisses were (gladly) received.

And after what in some ways seemed like a long while and in others a mere blink in time, they were wives.

The party adjourned to a restaurant in Bridgehampton for the wedding breakfast. There was the requisite white Rolls with streamers for the newlyweds and a line of more mundane though very expensive cars followed. As Bridget and Evelyn entered the restaurant, people in their Hamptons summer attire gawked and smiled and took impromptu photos on their phones and the group enjoyed the day. Simply. As the brides wished.

Peter and Amy further insisted on taking care of the honeymoon. First-class to London. The Belgravia house was at their disposal, fully staffed like an episode of *Upstairs Downstairs*. They had a blast. Through her Metropolitan Museum contacts, Bridget arranged for private tours of parts of both the National Gallery and the Tate Modern and they spent one evening at a gallery opening in the West End. Evelyn found a local running club for a run to and around Hampstead Heath, regaling them with tales of her own Central Park runs.

They found a different small restaurant near Peter's townhouse each night and discovered each other anew again. And fell in love with each other again.

On the Thursday night, they ventured into a lesbian bar near Regent's Park that an English teammate recommended to Evelyn. It was the first time in such a place for both of them. They had a ball. When word got around the joint that they were married FOR LESS THAN A WEEK!, they were the subjects of several toasts.

Ms. Casey-Manners and Ms. Manners-Casey—as they would forever hold themselves out—danced with other women. Slow or fast, it didn't matter.

At one point they were approached by a butch who asked if they were both interested in having some real fun, an offer they politely declined. In the black cab back to the house, they debated which of them this Madeline was *really* interested in and had a good laugh and agreed to repeat the bar hopping experience when they returned to Manhattan.

They had told the staff that Peter had arranged to be there for this honeymoon that they'd be late that night and not to wait up, but one of the maids was ready for them as they came through the door. And they were glad of it, neither of them being particularly sober when they entered the foyer.

That, however, was not too great an obstacle for their determination. They got precious little sleep that night. Not because they weren't too tired. Because they were otherwise engaged. In the amazingly comfortable bed. They lay on their sides, spending what seemed like hours exploring each other until each had one of their special, intense orgasms.

When Evelyn woke up, Bridget was asleep and very peaceful in being so. She was also naked. Her wife took this as an invitation that created the opportunity to awaken her with her tongue. When Bridget was fully conscious and aware and extremely happy with her wife's method, she soon returned the favor by kneeling in front of Evie in the shower with its rainforest head that seemed to be the size of a margherita pizza.

That final night, Peter had arranged through the staff for a sumptuous dinner and dessert to be delivered and laid out so the newlyweds could spend the evening at the house and in the bed.

Before they went to sleep that final night, Evelyn stepped behind Bridget when her lover was about to brush her teeth. She ran her hand beneath Bridget's robe and up her legs. Bridget spread them and it took little time for her dearest Evelyn to push her to a climax, all the while with their eyes locked in the mirror.

Whatever feelings she had for Evie before paled in light of what she felt for her at those sweet and tender moments. Perfection. Mutual perfection.

Evelyn returned the favor, although in a slightly different manner. Having yet again fully exhausted their still young bodies and souls, they locked their eyes in the bathroom mirror. Evie tried to hide the smile and Bridget said, "fuck you for being able to do what you do to me" and then she quickly turned so that they could kiss yet again.

You. Do. Something. To me.

Evelyn smiled as she pinched her wife's cheek.

In a flash, they had their arms around each other, and each told the other that she loved her more than she ever thought it was possible to love another, and Evie held Bridget to her chest as her wife began to sob.

They slept sleeps not of the innocent but of the wholly contented.

In the morning, a cloudy, overcast one, they sat in the large kitchen with its French doors that opened to the intricate garden that they hoped to be able to lounge in when they next visited and had cereal and coffee.

After a final mutual, enjoyable shower under that rainforest head, they took a black cab to Heathrow.

As they flew home to JFK that morning on British Airways, they were in first-class seats that faced one another. It was, they knew, excessive, and they felt a little guilty about taking advantage of Peter's wealth. But not too guilty.

They savored the ability to simply be able to look at each other now and then during the flight as they otherwise read. And when the car dropped them off at their apartment on Saturday afternoon, they were never so glad to be home. There would be no carrying-across-the-threshold. They were equals.

And they were home.

21.

A COUPLE OF WEEKS after they returned from their honeymoon, the newlyweds were in the Hamptons house for the first time since the wedding. And only the second time since the *incident* between Evelyn and the long-gone Todd. They'd slept well and were a tangle of young love when they'd awakened, first Bridget, who remained in a stupor with an arm around Evelyn's waist, and then Evelyn herself.

When they got downstairs for breakfast, they saw a concerned Amy sitting at the kitchen island. She was alone. When the two sat across from her, Amy said "I need to speak with you about something." The two wives looked at one another then back to their host.

"It's *embarrassing.* I know she's been very good to you. But sometimes you have to suck it up and move on."

This made no sense.

They watched as Amy rose and opened a drawer beneath the counter. She took out a small box and passed it to Evelyn who opened it. Inside were two BMW fobs.

"God, Amy. You and Peter have done too much already."

"We just want you to be as safe as can be. We insist."

After they had gone to bed, a dark blue BMW 5 series with tan leather interior and all the fixin's had been parked in the driveway. Its license plate: "BCANDEM." *Bridget Casey and Evelyn Manners.* "Alphabetical," said Amy from behind. It wouldn't entirely accurate since each had officially added a hyphen and the other's surname. Otherwise, it was perfect. When the girls approached, they saw a baby seat in the back. Suddenly Amy came out carrying Petey.

"Let's take it for a spin." And the four of them drove to Montauk Point and back, and when they pulled into the pebbled driveway in East Hampton, the girls agreed to keep it, neither wishing to insult the giver by refusing.

Evelyn's treasured maroon 5 series was inherited by Bridget's folks.

22.

MAYBE THE MOST SURPRISING and perhaps miraculous thing of all was the connection that developed between Evie and Eve. Perhaps it was their names. Perhaps it was their natures. Somehow Evie became Eve's first grown-up friend.

It happened at the house. It was mid-July, the afternoon of the day the new BMW appeared. Evelyn was alone on the deck, under the umbrella and gazing at the waves as she was wont to do.

Eve had free rein of the house, of course. She ran onto the deck and saw Evelyn doing nothing. She sat on the lounge next to Evie.

"Whatch you doin'?"

Evelyn turned. "I like to watch the waves come in." Instead of seeing them move away as she had so often done, she saw them now as moving towards her, like the days she hoped to spend with Bridget. Days uncountable.

"Can I watch too?"

Evie moved over a bit and patted her lounge. Eve squished in as far as she could but there wasn't enough room. The adult grabbed the child and unceremoniously plopped her on her lap then without a thought wrapped her arms around the youngster's waist, pulling her against herself. The two sat for a minute or two.

"Too hot," Eve said and jumped up.

"How about a walk on the beach?" Evie asked.

All of this was happening spontaneously to Evelyn. She was not particularly fond of children. At least someone else's children, more and more knowing that she and Bridget would someday have at least one of their own. Were you to have asked her an hour earlier whether she could tolerate let alone actually enjoy one sitting on her lap, she would look at you like you had two heads. She would have wished the child gone as soon as possible. Now she was volunteering to go for a walk with one.

Eve ran inside, calling to her mother, "Mommy, I go to the beach with the pretty lady." Evelyn heard.

Fran grabbed her daughter's hand and led her to Evie. "She has a name, Eve. What's her name?"

"Eve Two." Whether she meant it as "Eve Too" or "Eve Two," no one ever discovered. From that moment on, Evelyn was "Eve 2" in the house.

Eve 1 and Eve 2 climbed down all thirty steps of the staircase that led from the side of the deck to the beach. Eve 2 held Eve 1's left hand while her right stabilized her on the banister. They sat on the bottom step and took off their sandals, which they placed neatly beside them.

"Ready?" Evie asked when she got up, and Eve nodded, said "ready," and stood, reaching for her new friend's hand. They turned right on the sand, to the west, and held hands as they began their initial journey.

Eve loved to talk, and slowly Evie discovered that she actually enjoyed listening to the girl's ramblings, like some Woolfian stream of consciousness with the magic of being from a little and very observant girl who liked to listen to her own voice. Evelyn found that Eve's talking was a comfort. She moved from the occasional *that's-nice* and *I-see* and soon was actually interactive. Eve once or twice tried to pull Evie to the water and the older woman surprised herself yet again by enjoying the little splashes the pair shared at the water's edge, in the slight ocean waves that kissed the sand when their journey from who-knows-where was exhausted before retreating whence they'd come.

233

They lost track of time. When Evelyn looked at her watch, she saw they had been gone for over twenty minutes. She didn't have her phone. Fran would be worried.

"Eve, we've got to head back. Let's run."

And the two turned and started running easily along the line where the water hit the beach, still laughing and holding hands, swinging their arms rhythmically with each step, Eve's two to Evie's one. But they quickly became well coordinated in this unusual pairing until, after a minute or so, Eve complained of being too tired and they were again walking.

About five minutes later, they saw a woman waving. Fran. When Eve recognized her, she ran ahead, breaking Evelyn's hold and screaming, "Mommy, Mommy." Evie jogged behind her.

"I'm sorry." Evie said to Eve's mother in a tone that neither could have imagined not too long before. "I lost track of time."

"We were having fun, Mommy."

Fran reached over and touched Evelyn's arm. "Thank you. I hope you wore her out."

"More like she wore *me* out."

And the three headed back slowly and contentedly, Eve in the middle and each woman holding one of her hands.

Lunch was ready when they got to the house—each member of the *family* was tasked with making lunch or dinner while out there or with clean-up, with those getting the groceries rotating. Since Evelyn was, um, not a good cook, she usually was assigned lunch.

Today was Peter's turn but everyone knew he couldn't get it right without his wife's help and that he would just order pizza—Speeddial 7—if she wasn't there. Inside, there were sandwiches and chips and tortellini salad with iced tea. Amy had picked it all up in town. Everyone grabbed a plate, and they sat in the great room. It was a little warm to be sitting on the deck.

That night, Evelyn lightly tapped on Fran's door.

"Come in."

Fran was on the bed browsing on her tablet, wearing a nightie and panties. Evie was still wearing her shirt and shorts. Eve had gone to bed in her girlish room some hours before.

"Can I have her?"

"There are times when I'd say *yes* in a heartbeat. But this isn't one of them. You can borrow her from time to time though."

They both smiled. Again, the mood flowed with a natural ease of...friends. Evelyn asked if she could sit on the bed, and Fran nodded.

"I've never had the chance to speak with you alone until we talked on the beach. I guess all I want to say is that I'm sorry for what I did to your mom and you. I spoke to her about it, and I think we're good. What about you?"

Fran put her tablet to her side. She then reached for Evie's left hand. She ran a finger across the simple wedding band.

"I more than anyone know we all make mistakes. Look. What matters is what happens now. We've both been clean-and-sober figuratively at least for a while and we're both in good places.

"More, Eve's taken to you. I've never heard her go on about someone like she did about you. What did you do to her?"

"God, she's wonderful." This was music to the mother's ear, but Evie was being truthful. "I just lost myself with her. I've never been a fan of kids. I usually find them, well, annoying. But I enjoyed walking with her. I meant it when I asked about her. Only if she wants to."

"Oh. She wants to. How about the three of us go for a drive tomorrow?"

And thus it was agreed. Bridget was fine with it. It would be good for Evelyn to go out with someone else and Bridget, too, heard from Fran about how much Eve liked her wife.

It was a bit awkward the next day while Eve 1, Eve 2, and Fran were away after Amy, Peter, and Petey headed out for some sort of kids' thing in nearby Amagansett.

That left Jane with Bridget. Alone. Much as Bridget had been reintegrated into the family, Jane remained on its outskirts. She was older than everyone by nearly twenty years. Had been single for over that long and was recently shaken by what happened with Todd.

Jane was on the deck, and Bridget came out to sit with her. To see if some closure was possible. She wasn't sure.

"Why were you so fast to forgive her?" Jane asked when Bridget was settled in her lounge, speaking of Evelyn.

They were separated on the deck but close enough for Bridget to hear.

"I knew she did something horrible to you," the nurse said. "I guess as I think about it, I just knew that if I didn't catch her as she was falling, she'd be gone and I couldn't let that happen."

"Did you love her then?"

Bridget was quiet. Finally, with them both looking out towards the Atlantic, she said, "I did but I hadn't admitted it to myself yet. I wasn't thinking but realized that I would do anything to protect her, even if from herself and even if it meant losing what I had with Peter and the others, especially Petey."

She looked over at Jane, who returned the move.

The younger woman continued. "And I've never, not once, ever doubted my decision to go with her."

She laughed slightly. "I didn't even know that I was gay. I just know that there is the one person in the universe who I cannot live without and it is her."

Jane gave a smirk. "You sound like you're just trying to justify what you did in rushing to her."

Bridget shook her head. "No. That's not it. The easy thing, the comfortable thing was to just let her go. I mean, I barely knew her. I'd only spent a few days with her.

"She confessed to me what she'd done with Todd and then everything blew up the next morning when she confessed to you and took off. I knew she was going to do that. I actually told her that there was no chance with me unless she did that right off."

Jane was surprised. "I didn't know that. I thought she decided to do it on her own. This makes it less voluntary, doesn't it?"

"We'll never know what she would have done if I hadn't been in the picture. You're right. But knowing her as I do now, I'm pretty sure she would have told you. Maybe not that morning but eventually. She could never have carried the guilt for very long. She always understood that it was the worst thing she'd ever done in her life and, if it matters, she regretted it then and has regretted it every moment since."

Jane conceded that they'd plainly reached the time to let bygones be bygones if only for everyone involved. They again were looking out over the ocean. Bridget broke the silence.

"You've gone through a lot. I hope you can feel that way about someone."

"I thought I did," said Jane, "and I was wrong twice." She couldn't hide the edge to her voice.

"I know how hard it was for *you* to forgive her," Bridget said, "and I can't tell you how happy she is that you did. Especially for me. I dreaded missing out on

Petey's birthday, and you made that possible. Look at Evie with Eve. But I can't tell you you'll get hit by lightning the way I blessedly was. I just hope you do. And in the end, that's why I forgave her."

Bridget was surprised when she felt Jane's hand touch hers. She didn't move it. She continued. "And I love her. And I don't think she'll do anything like that again. I still don't know why she did it. I don't think she does either. She says it was because she was...desperate for a man—ironic isn't it, given what happened?—and that it wasn't personal to Todd or you."

Their positions had become uncomfortable, physically at least. They again sent their gazes across the broad expanse of the ocean.

After another pause, Bridget resumed. "We don't need to buy that though. Maybe she was trying to prove she wasn't who she is. You know, what she was feeling about me. But I do know that she won't do anything like that again. If I didn't know that, I don't know whether I could love her. And I love her."

The two were again quiet.

Jane broke the silence. "I'm happy for you. I really am. I'm just jealous about it though."

They were silent for a while until the spell was broken by Jane getting up and asking Bridget if she wanted anything. Bridget thanked her and said *no*, and Jane said she was heading up to take a nap.

Alone, Bridget went down the stairs to the beach. As she stepped to the waterline and let the warm salty ocean caress her feet, she thought about the conversation. She knew she couldn't get sucked into being a matchmaker for Jane and she didn't want to become her confidante. But she was glad she got to talk about Evelyn as she had and that the talking helped her understand more about both of them. Thoughts she never articulated. They merely reinforced her desire and need and love for her wife.

She had not strayed far from the stairs when she heard Evelyn hailing her. She stopped and waved. When Evelyn got to her after her descent to the beach, they hugged each other tightly and turned to head back to the house.

As always, their hands were interlaced and their arms were swinging while Bridget gave the short version of her conversation with Jane.

"Little by little," she said, "I think we're making progress."

"That's all we can ask for," Evelyn wife said.

Bridget squeezed Evie's hand and together they turned to go up all of those thirty steps to the house to prepare for dinner.

23.

OVER THAT SUMMER, Bridget and Evelyn went out to East Hampton every three or four weeks. They had an open invitation and a room dedicated to them with a very comfortable bed. Still, they tired of the schlep to get there and the schlep to get back. Plus, they spent a few days at the memorable AirBnB in the Berkshires they'd enjoyed in February, the vacation where the fateful proposal was made, the one where their parents applauded that they'd finally gotten around to it.

They met Barry on one of their trips to East Hampton. It was the second time he'd come as Fran's guest and her secret roomie. They liked him very much and saw how he had done wonders for Fran.

When Fran was out on the beach with the two Eves, and Peter and Amy were out shopping with Petey for kids' stuff, Bridget sat with Fran's beau on the deck savoring the (literally) million-dollar view. They got along very well, in part delving into some of the minutia of Barry's company's product. Bridget has signed off on the Foundation's investment in it.

Then the conversation skewed into bits and pieces of Bridget's own life, a life that had become a wee bit complicated since that night she'd gotten a selfie with *the* Peter Edgar as a lark at the Lenox Hill benefit on 57th Street.

As happened upon Evelyn's first encounter with her, Bridget found that Barry had no trouble talking about himself and especially about some of the rocky times with Fran.

When the conversation turned toward Barry and some of the rough patches that had occurred between him and his girlfriend, he said, taking a long drink of his iced tea from his glass as he looked out to the watery horizon, "I think we've largely gotten over them."

He put the glass down and turned back to Bridget. "So things are good." He lightly banged his fist on the wood armrest of his Adirondack chair with a *knock wood*.

Bridget was glad to see that at least Fran might be beginning to have the stability in her own life that she could have, perhaps, had with Peter had she not succumbed to her greed and grabbed the opportunity that appeared after Bridget took her to Peter's place and introduced the two.

Bridget and Barry had both retreated into their own thoughts when they heard Eve's "We're back Auntie Bridget" from the stairway to the beach. They got up to see the gang of returnees climbing those stairs and before they reached the top, Bridget told Barry that she was very happy to have made his acquaintance.

* * * *

Still, pleasant as the days spent in Hamptons luxury was, nothing truly compared to Bridget's and Evelyn's weekend days at home in their little space in Manhattan. Each one rolled into simple and wonderful routines.

Rain or shine, Evelyn got up at about 7:30 and went for a run with her clubmates or ran a race in the Park. She was getting pretty good at it.

If she was not standing near the finish of a race growing hoarse in shouting encouragement to her wife as she neared the finish line, Bridget had coffee ready when she got home to the apartment, and Evie picked up a couple of bagels before she entered the building.

The simple ability to sit in on a Saturday morning and hop the subway to the Village or the bus across town or drive into the country in the new but still expensively garaged BMW or to see their folks was good.

As was, well, the shower.

It wasn't large, especially compared to the one in Peter's house in London, but that didn't matter. The bed wasn't large either but it had always been and they knew it would continue to be just the right size for them, whether at night or after they'd shared a good *wash* after one of Evelyn's runs or races.

It was all they wanted to do. Pleasure each other. It had become routine, yes, but as Evelyn found with her running, each time had its own magic.

24

ONE MORNING IN SEPTEMBER, Bridget received Evelyn's call a little after eleven. Dennis, Evelyn's father, was dead. A massive heart attack.

Bridget cabbed from her office to the hospital on the East River where she found Evie and her mom, Irene, stunned on a sofa in a waiting room. When Evelyn saw her, she rushed to Bridget as Irene remained sitting and gazing into space. All Evelyn could do was to alternate between saying *Dennis* and asking *Why?* Again and again. *Dennis. Why?*

Irene was staring into a place no one should have to go. The girls took seats on either side of her and Bridget wrapped her arm around her mother-in-law. Two or three people from Evie's dad's office were milling around in shock. He was walking, one of them said, in the hallway to his office with his coffee. Nothing unusual until he stopped and collapsed. EMTs were on the scene within fifteen minutes but it didn't matter.

Of all her skills, comforting the bereaved was among Bridget's least favorite, but she was good at it. She pulled Irene to her and let the older woman cry into her shoulder while a numb Evelyn took the seat on Irene's other side, holding her mom's hands. It was a too-frequent reminder to the former nurse of the limits of what she could do.

After some minutes, Bridget got up and found a hospital staffer. She explained that she was the decedent's daughter-in-law and an RN. She confirmed the logistics of what would happen next. She asked that she be the family's liaison, which Evie said was okay, and then arranged for a car to take her with Evelyn and Irene home to Chappaqua. On the way, she called her own mom, an active nurse, and asked that she come up if she could and that she tell her father what happened.

Two hours later, Irene was fitfully sleeping in her, and her late husband's, bed. Evie sat on the sofa downstairs with Bridget and Bridget's mother, Astrid, on either side of her.

"I was just turning into someone," Evelyn got out between gasps, "he'd be proud of after so long. I was such a disappointment—"

"Whatever you had been, Evelyn, he saw the new you." This was Astrid interrupting her daughter-in-law's honest recital. "He couldn't stop talking about how wonderfully you were doing, how much Bridget made you happy. He could barely contain his excitement that night in Massachusetts when Bridget proposed. And again at the wedding. He so loved you. And he was so proud of the woman you've become."

"Thank you, Mrs. Casey, thank you," Evelyn stuttered somewhat awkwardly since neither she nor Bridget were yet able to refer to their in-laws by their first names.

Evelyn's brother, Jess, got to Chappaqua on a red eye the day after their father died. He helped both women in the first hours and went through some of his dad's things with his sister. Evie and Irene could never have made it through without him, even though he had to head back west five days after the funeral.

25.

FOR ABOUT A MONTH, Evelyn spent at least one weekend night at the Chappaqua house. Usually both. Bridget sometimes didn't accompany her. She and Evelyn agreed that it was important that the Manners women spend some time alone.

Once a week, Irene stopped at the girls' place for dinner, usually at the apartment but sometimes at a restaurant, before taking a cab to get the train home. These visits helped her recovery and the handling of the unimaginable grief, as did throwing herself too much into her work.

Irene was embarking on a long grieving period, moving slowly but with the help of her immediate and extended family and work colleagues through its stages.

That help was spectacularly on display on a late Thursday afternoon about two months after the death. It was about five that afternoon when Irene looked up upon hearing a knock on her open office door.

Standing in a beautiful, burgundy gown was Astrid Casey. Astrid, a Swede, looked to have just gotten off a runway. Tall and slim with beautiful but short blonde hair and impeccable makeup and only a few pieces of fine jewelry. Although she didn't look entirely comfortable in the gown, she pulled it off like a natural.

Astrid had a garment bag over her arm. Before Irene could say a word, she stepped in and closed the door.

"We're going to a party," she said sternly. "You need to be dressed properly." Irene's tailored dark-blue suit with ivory blouse apparently wouldn't do. Astrid placed the bag on the hook on the door and unzipped it. It exposed a midnight-blue gown. The lawyer looked from it to the nurse and back.

"Hello, Astrid. Nice to see you. What the hell are you talking about?"

"Bridget and Evelyn, thanks to Peter and Amy, are taking both of us to a small gala at the Metropolitan."

"Opera?"

"Art."

"I can't possibly—"

Astrid held her palm out to stop anything more coming from the sudden widow. "You can and you will."

"But shoes?" Her hands pointed towards the sensible pumps on her feet.

Astrid opened the door and stuck her head out.

"Girls," and the word was still in the air when the girls—both in their own gowns—came in, Evelyn with a shoebox and a bag from Azaleas, a lingerie boutique in the East Village, and Bridget with a jewelry box. Evelyn had secretly borrowed one of her mom's old gowns as a template for this one's measurements.

For the next fifteen minutes, with the blinds down on the window that was next to the office door, Irene was transformed. By this time, most of those on Irene's floor had gotten wind of what was happening, and a cheer broke out when the door to her office was opened and every lawyer and staff member nearby was waiting. The old lawyer emerged and nervously and wobbly headed with the other three to the elevator.

A black Escalade awaited them on Sixth Avenue. When the four women in evening gowns emerged from the building, quite the incongruous site, the driver jumped to open the back door for three of them while Bridget was content with the passenger's seat up front.

They drove over to Madison and then north and then west to Fifth and pulled up right in front of the grand entrance to the museum. Peter and Amy were waiting on the sidewalk. As the Cadillac slowed to a stop, Peter stepped to open the back door while Amy did the same with the front. Tight hugs were exchanged, particularly tightly for a still shocked Irene Manners.

They went in together. In the museum's grand entryway, they were met by a curator who led them off to the side and into a room with a cavernous ceiling that was arranged for a cocktail service. The museum itself was closed. But not to them.

Amy said that they were there for an event that began at seven but that thanks to some string-pulling, they had the place largely to themselves until then. Astrid had volunteered to show them some of her favorite displays.

For a glorious hour, the six savored several of the museum's nineteenth- and twentieth-century galleries under Astrid's expert guidance.

When they got to the formal festivities in the museum's large ballroom, they found Bridget's dad Danny waiting nervously by the sign-in table. Of them all, he was by far the most uncomfortable in his formal wear but Peter did his best to put him at ease. They mingled for cocktails and enjoyed the evening, and when it was over and the attendees were streaming out, Irene, Evelyn, and Bridget took a car to Chappaqua, each feeling like Cinderella.

They would have felt a bit guilty about it, but after Irene started up the stairs with a *Now you girls be good* and stopped after three steps and turned back to them and added, *quietly* and displayed perhaps the first smile she had since her husband died, the girls knew she was on the mend.

More immediately they knew that their hormones would get to play without a chaperone.

The two had been pawing each other all night in their fancy outfits and tingling lingerie. At dinner, Astrid asked Irene if they should separate their daughters, who then promised to *be good*. And they tried to but didn't always succeed.

When they heard Irene's door close at the house, they walked up the stairs. The two had slept together in the house several times over the prior months but had done nothing beyond cuddling even after they were married. Maybe a little rubbing, too. They were well past that that night.

After each went to the bathroom, they reconvened in the bedroom, still in their gowns. Bridget's was golden and Evelyn's silver. They received more than a few glances at the gala. From men *and* from women. They hadn't noticed. Now they saw what everyone had been gawking at. Now they stepped back after a kiss, each to take in the view of the other. They often did this when they were naked. This was the first time they were dressed so formally. They felt like Bond Girls.

They were strangely nervous. It had been a spectacular evening, better than either had hoped after Amy had suggested it. Amy had gotten them to accept the gowns, and those for their mothers and the tux for Bridget's dad, and the rest as yet another wedding present.

But all of the things that had been bought paled when compared with the feeling they got to share with their mothers and the art they got to enjoy together and intimately. And no amount of money would be enough to pay for the knowing smile that Irene had given them as she went up the stairs.

But that was too cerebral. As the two stood with their eyes roaming up and down, the separation couldn't last long. And it didn't.

Soon, after the gowns were discarded with little of the care they deserved, the pair became wonderfully engaged. It took little time and effort from Bridget for Evie's shaking to become uncontrollable, and uncontrolled. Her body was transformed into nothing but a vessel for the passion she felt at her lover's touch, by lips and by fingers.

When she was done, Bridget gently pushed Evelyn back on the bed. Before Bridget could lie next to her, Evie began to cry. She had cried many times since her father died. She would never understand why he was taken so young but she was getting used to the rawness of her feelings. The rawness of her lover and the rawness of her loss collided in the room in the house where she had grown up. And where her father should be sleeping twenty feet away and her mother should be in bed with her father twenty feet away.

Evie heaved as Bridget comforted her. As they were both beginning to get chilled, Bridget got up and pulled an oversized T-shirt from one of Evelyn's drawers and helped her put it on. It frightened Bridget, seeing this precious being go from ecstasy to despair so quickly.

She didn't expect this change in Evelyn. It was as if a trap door had sprung and she was standing on the floor watching Evie fall helplessly into the abyss. *Had I not been paying attention? Had I not understood the extent to which Evelyn was suppressing her feelings about her father?*

Bridget was chilled by the realization. When she fell asleep, she had no answers to her own questions.

26.

THE ALARM WOKE THEM both at 6:30 the next morning. They had to go to work. At some point during the night, Bridget had turned so her naked ass was butting against Evie's naked ass. Neither had the wherewithal or, frankly, the incentive to do anything about it. Any hopes of sleeping a bit longer were dashed when they heard a sharp knock on the door.

Irene said, "are you decent?" as she opened it. "We have an 8:21 train to catch and I need to get a cab because my car was left at the station after your little stunt." She smiled when the two told her to leave them alone. "Gear up at eight."

Irene had never seen them in bed together. They had morning hair and were grouchy but they were a couple. As she headed downstairs, she didn't dare think what their hands were doing at that moment. She had heard one of them come during the night—so much for her request that it be done *quietly*—but also heard Evelyn's wailing. It broke her heart but she knew the one person that could deal with it better than she could was with her.

How wonderfully things had gone, excepting for that horrible detour of Dennis's death, since that day when the two held hands as they walked to the house that first time.

In fact, the girls were awkward with each other when they awoke, lying silently with their thoughts and hands grasped together.

"You okay?" Bridget asked when her mother-in-law had left them.

Evelyn flipped so she could face Bridget.

"I don't know what came over me," she said as her wife ran a finger across her cheek before leaning forward to give her a light kiss.

"You've been going through stuff no one deserves to go through. I am here for you."

Evelyn nodded. "I know."

"You okay?" Bridget repeated.

"As long as you promise to be patient with me."

Bridget gave her wife another light kiss.

"I promise."

Evelyn sighed. "Now we'd better get up or we'll both feel the Wrath of Irene which, from personal experience, I can assure you, you do not want to have to face."

And they got up and were ready when the car pulled in front of the house at eight to take them to the train. They wore slacks and polo shirts and sneakers and would change into what they wore yesterday when they got to their offices.

They were in Grand Central within an hour.

27

THERE WAS NO PRECIPITATION and the temperature rose into the low-40s for Christmas Eve. At about one, Evelyn double-parked the new BMW in front of the apartment, and she and Bridget put several bags into the trunk. A box of baked goods the two made the night before was delicately placed on the back seat.

They got on the FDR Drive at 96th Street. Traffic on I-87 and the parkways was light. They made it to Chappaqua in under an hour. Truth be told, Evelyn loved feeling the power of the new car and the way it handled. They sang along with the carols that sprung from the fancy sound system and arrived at Irene's in no time.

For her part, Irene found the empty house often haunted by her memories of her husband and of raising her children and the family had begun to speak of downsizing. They knew that this would likely be their last Christmas there. Jess had come to New York for Thanksgiving and was coming again.

The girls were maintaining their bi-weekly trips to the house and, with a few exceptions, Irene was still having dinner with them in the city once a week. The progress, especially after the Metropolitan Gala, was remarkable. Irene was alive again. Everyone knew she would never get over losing Dennis. She had, though, come to accept it, the final stage of the process of living on after the death of her husband. The dinners were no longer attempts at recovery. They were simply something people who love each other and enjoy each other's company do.

Irene was in high spirits when the girls came in that Christmas Eve. She was wrapping some last-minute gifts near the tree the three of them had bought and decorated the prior Sunday. It was a bit smaller than Dennis would have picked out, somehow locked into the notion that size mattered. It was plenty big enough and perfect for the space in the corner of the living room.

They'd offered to pick Jess up at JFK, but he insisted that he could get to the house on his own. And he did.

They'd be joined on Christmas itself by a throng, consisting of the Edgars and the Caseys and even Fran, Jane, Eve, and Barry. Then it'd be bedlam.

But now, on December 24, Jess had gotten himself settled into his old room and the others sat in the kitchen, doing some final prep work for the holiday. The kitchen had been redone about five years earlier. It had an Aga stove and a Sub-Zero refrigerator and freezer. The key change, though, was the creation of a marble-top island with a row of stools. It was the de facto informal center of the house, and Evelyn and Bridget sat there until Irene reminded them that they too had work to do. Jess came down and was assigned his own tasks.

Once the clock struck four, Irene made gin-and-tonics for each of them and they adjourned to the living room. Evelyn sat on the sofa with Bridget perpendicular to her so her legs crossed Evie's. Jess sat on one armchair at an angle to the sofa and Irene was in the other. They both loved watching the two women. Irene's feet were on the coffee table, next to Evelyn's, their legs lightly touching. Some jazzy Christmassy songs were coming through the Bluetooth speaker.

In the quiet, Evelyn finally told her mother that she and Bridget knew there would come a time but they weren't yet ready to have a baby. Hearing her daughter say this made Irene smile. She wasn't ready to be a grandmother just yet.

Then she stood, collected their glasses, and went to get everyone a refill.

THE END

About the Author

JOSEPH P. GARLAND is a native New Yorker. He grew up in Tuckahoe, New York, the village to the north of Bronxville and now lives in Mount Vernon, the city to the south of Bronxville. He is a lawyer, now living in Westchester County. He has a BA from Manhattanville College in Purchase, New York and a JD from Columbia Law School in Morningside Heights, Manhattan.

Excerpts from all of his works can be found at DermodyHouse.com/books.

Other Novels

Contemporary

I Am Alex Locus is set largely in Bronxville but mostly on the Upper West Side. It is the story of a twenty-three-year-old woman who fortuitously discovers that he deceased mother was a writer. Alex goes through her mother's stories to try to learn the truth about her family. And she does, although it is not always as pleasant as she had been led to believe.

My Husband's Daughter: Discovering Scarlet Evans is also set largely in Bronxville, where a 16-year-old stranger is waiting at Cassandra Owens's front door one day with a letter, a letter that reveals that she, Scarlet Evans, is the daughter of Cassandra's late husband. Thus begins a story of Cassandra trying to make peace with the girl as she tries to move on from her late husband's deceit,

The Early Gilded Age

Garland's first Gilded Age novel is *Róisín Campbell*. It is the story of Róisín Campbell, who comes from County Limerick in 1870 and goes from being a maid to being a nurse and the mother of her late sister's son.

He has also written *A Studio on Bleecker Street* and *A Maid's Life*. These are literary novels set in the 1870s, chiefly in New York City and have intersecting stories, with Róisín Campbell being the first of them. A fourth book, *Disfigured*, is in its final stages of production.

Jane Austen Fan Fiction

He has also written three *Pride and Prejudice* Variations. The first, *Becoming Catherine Bennet*, tells the story of what happens to Catherine/Kitty Bennet after she is allowed to join her sister Lydia with Mr. Wickham in Newcastle (contrary to what Miss Austen says happens to her).

The Omen at Rosings Park imagines a world in which Elizabeth Bennet says "yes" to Mr. Collins. Both are available on Kindle Unlimited as well as ebooks and paperbacks.

The Colonel and Miss Bennet follows Colonel Fitzwilliam to Waterloo and afterward, ultimately to be loved by one of the Bennet sisters.

A *Persuasion* sequel, *The Diary of Elizabeth Elliot* tells the story of what happened to Elizabeth Elliot her sister and her cousin and her companion left Bath at the end of that novel.

Many of these books are available on Kindle Unlimited.

Romances by J.P. Garland

Coming to Terms (FF and MF)*
Disowned (FF)
An Historian on Oxford's High Street (MF)
A Theory About Valentine's Day (FF)
On Finding Love and Acceptance (FF)
A Fairytale of New York (MF)
My London Honeymoon (FF)
The Sergeant and the Suspect (FF)
Matty Troy and Me (MF)
The Vintage Gown (FF)
Iubirea Mea (My Love) (FF)

*MF=Male Female Romance
FF=Female Female Romance

DERMODYHOUSE.COM